Deep in the Woods

A Thriller

Mica Merrill Rice

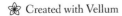 Created with Vellum

For my sons, Gabriel and Cameron. Never stop chasing your dreams. I love you both!

Chapter One

November, 2004

This can't be my life, Ella thought to herself. She buzzed around the house deep in thought while her son, Brandon, sat in front of the fireplace with Bella, the black Lab given to her by her Zach. Brandon played with his toy phone and pretended to make calls as she picked up toys and cleaned up the table from dinner. Bella slept peacefully, happy to have a break from playing with a toddler, of that Ella was sure.

How can I even do this alone? A question she had grappled with over the last few weeks swirled in her head like a tornado. She continued to fight with her thoughts when Alice's voice gently dropped in.

"Let me help you, dear." Alice scooped Brandon off the floor. "I can give him a bath for you." And without allowing Ella time to protest, she carried him off to the bathroom to fill the tub, talking to Brandon along the way as they discussed what bubbles they might use and if Brandon preferred his yellow duck tonight over the tiny water boat toy.

1

Ella managed a tired smile as she watched them walk away. Alice had stayed by her side from the minute he was born, even though her own son, Zach, was gone.

Her heart ached. Zach was gone. Ella still had a difficult time wrapping her head around it.

Her emotions were draining her both mentally and physically. If she had any energy left from the day, she burned it running the house and taking care of her son. Despite the exhaustion, she didn't mind. He was all she had left of Zach, all of the life she once loved so dearly, and she would go to the ends of the earth to provide for him. She put her head in her hands and slumped her shoulders. Never in a million years would she have seen herself here, raising Brandon without Zach by her side.

Her wounds still felt fresh from that horrid day. A permanent scar etched into her memory that could never heal.

It had happened over Fourth of July weekend, and there was much to celebrate. The Stones loved to host friends and family at the farm. They would bring tents and camp out for days on end, so the smells of campfire would permeate the air. Kids would run around laughing as they twirled their sparklers like stars in the night. Guests would beat the daytime heat by cooling down in the pond that sat downhill from the main house.

But none of that would happen that weekend.

The first guest to arrive that day was the town sheriff. Ella recalled laughing at something (probably an old story Alice was telling her of Zach as a child—she loved to share stories of him growing up there on the farm), as they put the last-minute décor on the front porch when the patrol car approached the house. At first, she thought nothing of it, but when the officer exited his vehicle with a solemn look upon his face, she knew his news was dire.

"Ella..." He hesitated, looking down at the ground and holding his hat in his hands. "I'm afraid I have some bad news."

"What do you mean?" Ella felt her heart plummet. She already knew what was coming but had to hear it for herself.

"There's been a hunting accident, Ella." The sheriff ran his fingers along the brim of the hat. He couldn't bear to look her in her eyes. "We found Zach dead in the woods from an apparent gunshot wound to the head."

Those words and the words that followed changed everything she knew in an instant. The baby growing inside her at the time would never know his father. They would never embark on the journeys they had planned. Forever was gone as quickly as the words had fallen from the officer's mouth, and almost two years later, her wounds from that day still felt fresh.

Tears filled the pockets in her eyes as she found herself now getting ready to marry Jimmy, their best friend, and feeling an overwhelming sense of loneliness. If it were not for Alice to keep her going, she would have run away and hid herself away in the shadows. The love she shared with Zach could not be matched, and the guilt she felt for agreeing to marry Jimmy, haunted her like a never-ending nightmare.

Jimmy had been so good to her and Brandon, providing

her with strength she no longer possessed. She gazed at the engagement ring that sat on her wedding finger. To her, it felt like nothing more than a piece of unceremonious metal. She felt no connection to it or to Jimmy anymore, but it just seemed so natural at the time to say yes to him. To say yes to the support. To say yes to the man who had such a strong connection with Zach. And by marrying him, she could somehow keep those memories of Zach alive.

Squeezing her eyes shut and opening them again, she began her descent back down to reality, to the toddler she rocked in the dark, the dim light of the nightlight in his room illuminating his features. *Beautiful,* she thought to herself. His eyes twitched as he dreamed, seemingly without a care in the world.

"I love you, baby, forever and always," she whispered, leaning her head down to place a soft kiss on his warm forehead. She took in his scent, still fresh from his bath, and smiled. She found a sense of peace with him in her arms.

She sang her nightly lullaby to him, "Hush Little Baby," a ritual she conducted every night without exception, hoping one day he would remember those small moments they shared together.

His arm reached out to stretch and he yawned, a deep and relaxed breath. Ella raised herself out of the rocker with Brandon in her arms, laying him down in his crib for the night. She backed out of the room on tiptoes, carefully closing the door behind her, watching her son dream away as the door inched its way shut. She had so many aspirations for him, but nothing left for herself anymore. She allowed herself to draw in a deep breath and let it out slowly. Her dreams were buried with Zach, she thought to herself, and she must focus on Brandon, and only Brandon, from here on out.

She made her way to the living room and turned off the overhead lights, leaving only the glow from the fire in the fireplace. Bella was still curled up in her dog bed in front of the hearth, paying no mind to Ella, who had taken repose next to her. Ella looked at her and imagined what it must be like to be as relaxed and trusting as her faithful companion. She softly stroked her head between the ears as she planned her next steps. She needed to tell Alice that she intended to break her engagement to Jimmy. It was a painful task she dreaded and knew she had to do. She wondered what Alice would think. Ella had been hiding her feelings from everyone for months. Even from Jimmy. Alice was such a kind soul, but Ella worried the news would crush her in some way. Alice was so fond of Jimmy, and it seemed as though he filled the hole in her heart after the loss of Zach. Ella was certain that once she revealed her intentions, it would no doubt send shockwaves through her. He was like a second son to her and the only son she had left now. Ella hoped Alice would allow her and Brandon to stay at the farm, but she felt it may be awkward. She had to be prepared to leave and start over in a new place.

She felt the bile rising up in the back of her throat and she instinctively swallowed, pushing the anxiety back down to her gut. She got up and headed to the front door, stopping to look at the mess of a woman she had become. Her curly black hair tucked into a bun on her head like an abandoned bird's nest. Her mahogany eyes, which once sparkled with joy, seemed so dull now. Her eyes appeared sunken from the dark circles that surrounded them. She turned away, disgusted with herself for becoming such a train wreck.

She grabbed her keys, her purse, and headed out the door.

It was crisp and cool out, smells of burning wood flowing gently through the air. The full moon cast light on the property so brightly that she could make out the outlines of the trees that surrounded them. The leaves had fallen for the season, leaving the branches bare. It seemed eerie to her the way their long, jagged branches resembled that of a witch's pointy fingers, facing in every direction.

She headed down the front porch toward the driveway. The sound of her feet against the soft wood of the steps was interrupted with a rustling in the distance. She stopped and listened, her heart pounded a beat faster. *Who! Who!* The call of an owl echoed into the night. She watched as a Great Horned Owl flew out from the trees. She let out a sigh of relief and chuckled to herself. *Get a grip, Ella.*

As she approached her car, she heard the crackle of leaves in the distance. The crackle of footsteps. Immediately she froze, her body tingling with instant fear. She slowly turned her head to the direction of the noise, and before she could scream, he had come up behind her and placed his gloved hand over her mouth and wrapped his other arm around her body, the smell of leather and sweat filling her nostrils.

"Shhhhhhhh..." He tightened his grip around her waist. "Don't make a sound," he whispered in a frighteningly calm manner, his breath hot like an iron against her neck.

He brushed her neck with the cold, sharp edge of his knife.

Ella's eyes begin to tear, smelling his familiar scent. She nodded her head, indicating to her captor that she would remain dutifully silent.

"Why are you doing this to me?" she begged, her voice ragged with fear. "I...I just don't understand. I haven't done anything to you."

"Nothing?" he said as he let out a condescending chuckle. "Darling, you've done everything. You turned my entire world upside down from the minute you stepped foot in this town, and I want it back." He tightened his grip on her as the anger built inside of him.

He pushed her forward until she was pinned against her car, the weight of his body crushed her until she felt she could not breath. "Take this and write what I tell you." He slammed a wrinkled piece of paper in front of her and shoved a pen between her fingers. "I want you to write that you're sorry. Ask for forgiveness!"

Ella felt both petrified and confused but did as she was told. He held her hand as she wrote, his rotted breath just inches from her ear. "Here, I'm done," she said in a soft whisper, her voice shaking. She further tried to defuse the situation, sensing he was like a pot ready to boil over. "I'll give you whatever you want...no one has to know about tonight."

"It's too late!" he hissed as he forcefully turned her around to face her, gripping her shoulders and looking her in the eye.

Ella's eyes grew wide like that of a doe who has spotted her hunter. His eyes quickly panned down the front of her to her neck to the gold object that caught the light of the moon. His stern look swiftly morphed into a malicious smile as he noticed her crucifix.

He yanked it off her neck and examined it under the dim light of the moon, as if he were inspecting a foreign object. "The Lord giveth, and the Lord can taketh away." His tone was cold and matter-of-fact. "Where is your God now? Foolish woman! God doesn't answer prayers. You see, Ella," he continued, slowly moving around to her back, like a panther about to pounce his prey, "everything you have belongs to me, and I intend to take back what's mine."

Ella's heart pounded so fiercely she thought it may burst out of her chest. She dared not scream or he may not let her go, or worse, he would kill her and then her family just for spite. "Please," she begged, tears flowing down her cheeks, "don't do this."

"This is going to be far more enjoyable than I ever imagined," he said, ignoring her plea. "I am a hunter, Ella. I'll take you now, but I will wait for your son until he is full grown, that I promise you. I'm no baby killer, and besides, I want to enjoy the hunt for as long as I can."

He moved his hands to the front of her shirt, cupping her breast, as his breath changed to a slow and patient one. "Ah, yes, Ella...I'm gonna make sure the pain you feel now continues until I have what is mine."

He tugged at her jaw with his free hand, exposing her neck, and slit her throat across the front. Ella felt the warmth of her blood flowing down to her chest, leaving her powerless to make even a whimper. The pain began to sink in, and he let her go, her body falling lifeless to the ground.

She closed her eyes and said her last prayer silently as she lay there hoping God would hear her plea.

She opened her eyes one last time to see him standing over her with a cold smirk on his face. She drew her last breath. No one to hear her. No one there to change her fate as she slipped away into nothingness.

Chapter Two

Penn State University, 2024

Brandon's eyes slowly flittered open like the mechanical eyes of a toy doll. He peered up from his bed and out of the small dorm window to see a sky filled with puffs of steel-colored clouds and no sun in sight. This was the day he should be staying in and catching up for the history midterm coming up next week, but for now, he admitted to himself, the bed was much more appealing. He stretched under the warm, down comforter, thinking about what needed to be done for the day.

He glanced over to his roommate's empty bed and smiled. *Lucky bastard.* Steve was most likely at his girl-friend's apartment again. She was a senior living off campus and shacking up with Steve, who was a sophomore. Brandon woke up most mornings alone in his dorm, some-thing the boys on his floor envied, and Brandon didn't mind at all.

Brandon shifted his gaze to the ceiling and let his mind deconstruct the dream he had woken up from. He had always had the same dream ever since he could remember.

Always in a field somewhere, surrounded by tall blades of golden wheat. The field was considerable and flanked on all sides with trees from a forest, as tall as the sky. It was as if he was in a dome, but the roof was open to let the light in. In most of these bizarre dreams, he just lay in the wheat, looking up to the blue sky above, the sun shining on him, warming his body, no matter the season. Other times the sky was black, except for the brilliant light of the moon, which cast its soft light on the field, just enough for him to make out the trees enveloping the field. He never went anywhere, and no one ever came to see him. Occasionally, he found himself meandering aimlessly about the field, letting his hands glide over the tops of the wheat and taking in the fresh air. In there, he felt protected and never felt isolated. There was a presence there, he could feel it somehow surrounding him, holding him tight. Brandon knew this dream was not the norm, so he didn't share it with anyone, not even Maddie, his best friend.

But last night, the dream was different, and he considered breaking his promise to himself never to share that level of detail with anyone.

It began just as it usually did. He was standing in the field, the sun setting beyond the trees, which had shed their leaves in time for fall. He smelled the sweet smell of pine trees with the breeze that traveled through the field. The light wind moved the tops of the trees, and he could hear them creaking, just as an old rusty door would, as they moved back and forth. Then he noticed a structure in the distance, just past the tree line to the west. And although it was a clear evening, he wasn't able to make out the details. It was as if he were looking through the lens of a camera and the structure was set out of focus. It wasn't big enough to be a house, but what else could it be?

He had tried to walk toward the structure but found himself frozen and unable to move, his feet planted firmly in the ground. He remembered squinting his eyes to bring the structure into focus to no avail. Just as he was about to call out to see if anyone was with him, he awoke alone and warm in his bed, everything just as it was when he had fallen asleep the night before.

Brandon kicked the sheets off and rolled out of bed, grabbing his bathroom kit before heading to the shared bathroom space that joined his room to the one next door. His mind was consumed with the nuances of last night's dream. He stood hunched over the sink in front of the mirror, examining his face, and he began thinking of his mother. He had been told he looked like her by his stepdad, Jimmy, but that the height came from his father's side. At 6'4", he was no slouch, his hair a black curly mop, his skin bronze, and his eyes were green like the sea. All traits that he cherished from the parents he did not get to know.

Except for his mother.

Brandon knew no one would believe him if he told them, but he could still remember his mother. He was just two when she disappeared (though Jimmy still believed she ran away), but he could recall vividly every detail of her looks, her scent, and her sweet voice. No child that age could possibly remember those details, he was sure anyone would tell him as much, but he always felt he had some sort of gift. Perhaps that was a trait he inherited from her as well.

His last memory of her was the night she left.

A sudden wave of sadness washed over him, and his

heart ached at the thought of her. He splashed cold water on his face and tried to clear his thoughts. *Focus, Brandon!* But his thoughts were still heavy, and no amount of water could wash them away. He needed to confide in someone, and that someone would have to be Maddie. She was the only one he would trust with these details. With a plan in mind, he got himself in the shower and benched his thoughts for later in the day.

Later that day, Brandon found himself a seat in the corner of The Constant Brew, a small coffee shop not far from campus. It was their usual spot, a small table tucked next to the front window. A few leather couches adorned the reading room just off the main area, surrounded by shelves of books and games. It always smelled of fresh coffee and delectable pastries. The college-aged servers bustled about in their black pants and matching black shirts, most looking Goth-like, with their pale faces and Doc Martens. Brandon loved coming here to hang out and watch the goings-on. This was a popular spot for most students at the campus for the same reason.

He took a sip of his piping hot coffee, black with no cream or sugar, letting the warm liquid make its way from his throat and down through the middle of his body, as he patiently waited for his best friend to arrive.

Maddie had always been late from the day he met her, and Brandon was known to be routinely on time. An odd pair from the moment they met, he had met Maddie on the first day of the ninth grade. Brandon was on the bus headed to St. Christopher's Catholic School in King of Prussia. The bus driver made all the usual stops, picking up all the usual faces, but that morning they made a new stop at the corner of Felton and Cherry St. The bus stopped and opened its doors, but no one was there. The bus sat there for a few moments, the students seemingly unaware that anything was any different than the last stop. And then he saw her. This beautiful creature, with her wavy red hair and long legs running under her pleated, plaid uniform skirt. She jumped on the bus and came up the two steps, stopping only for a moment at the front before donning her confident smile, never even breaking a sweat or seeming to be out of breath from the dash through the streets. She captured the attention of every girl and boy alike as she strutted down the center aisle.

And then her eyes locked with Brandon's, this beautiful siren. He could only stare, his mouth partly open, captivated by her spell. She made her way to the back of the bus and sat next to him. What came next had been the greatest adventure of his life with his new best friend.

The sun was making its descent into darkness as Brandon watched Maddie strut her way down the block and into the front door of The Constant Brew. Brandon waved to her, and she turned to him with a familiar smile, as she began to unbutton the camel-colored wool coat and remove the knit hat, exposing her wavy, dark red locks. She walked over and gave Brandon a hug before taking the chair across from him.

The two picked up where they left off the previous day, catching up on the latest dorm scandals, upcoming midterms, and the much-anticipated Thanksgiving break. The waitress came over mid-conversation to take Maddie's order, a mocha latte, as usual. Maddie was not always predictable and loved to be the wild child, but one thing always remained the same, her choice in coffee.

"Where were we?" she asked, turning back to Brandon, as the waitress hurried off to get her drink, her hazel eyes looking at him through her long lashes.

"Maddie, I need to tell you something and I need your honest opinion," Brandon said, ready to rip the band-aid off on the latest dream. "But before I tell you," he said in a serious tone, "I need you to promise you won't laugh."

She giggled and caught herself when she realized he wasn't joking. "I promise I won't laugh. You can trust me."

Brandon began detailing his dream, taking care not to leave out any detail in case she picked up on any significance. She was meticulous about details, always insightful, and an incredible listener. He knew he could trust her with anything on his mind.

"Wait, wait, wait..." she said, waving her hands in front of her face. "You mean to tell me that you've had the *same* dream your whole life? Why are you just now telling me this?

"I mean, it's not the same dream." He suddenly felt embarrassed, his cheeks becoming flush with heat as if he just walked into a crowded room without pants. "Sometimes it is different. It can take place at night, other times during the day, seasons change."

"You realize people don't dream like this, not that I know of anyway. The fact that your dream is pretty much the same every night is pretty significant. Forget about the fact that there was a slight variation to it last night!"

"I dunno..." He briefly glanced down to his coffee, unable to look her in the eye for the moment. "I just have this weird feeling about this nuance. I've never seen anything other than the field and trees, and now, all of a sudden, I see something there, but I can't move."

"Maybe this dream is an attempt at sending you a message from beyond. It could also be nothing, you know," she said, trying not to alarm him. "Could just be stress. We have finals coming up, it's our senior year—"

"What's to stress about, Maddie? I've got the perfect life!" Brandon joked, sitting back his chair and folding his arms across his chest with a smile.

She knew his mom had disappeared without a trace when he was young, and he wasn't the type to have a mass of friends at school, by choice. He never wanted to be put in a position again where he would have to say goodbye and feel that pain, like the day he said goodbye to all of his childhood friends at the end of the third grade, after Jimmy informed them they had to leave the farm and move to a new city for a fresh start. That was a day he would never forget, and though he loved his stepdad, he never forgave him for taking him from the life he loved.

Life was a series of unfortunate events that led to chance encounters. He remembered that if it weren't for them moving out of that town, he would not have met Maddie.

"I don't think it's stress, Maddie."

"Well, if it were me, I would start by writing down whatever detail I had in a dream journal. Jot down things that are different and that stand out to you. You know? You may notice a theme or something. It could be the universe trying to tell you something, and the only way it knows to do this is through your bizarre dream."

Brandon felt comforted just getting it off his chest. She had a point. It could be a fluke, he thought for a moment, but he promised to write it all down so they could look at it together.

"You ready for tonight?" she asked, shifting the conversation again. Ethan Lopez, the quarterback for the college football team, was having a party for his girlfriend's birthday. It was to be the party of the year.

He nodded to her, and they formed their plans for later that evening, the worry Brandon had earlier in the day beginning to wane. He was looking forward to having a little fun with Maddie and could use the break from studies.

"Pick me up at nine?" she asked, as they stood up to gather their belongings and leave.

He nodded before leaning in for their hug, and then they walked their separate ways toward the campus to get ready.

Chapter Three

Brandon returned to his dorm room after dropping Maddie off at hers, feeling slightly buzzed from the alcohol he consumed at the party. The inevitable post-drink regret set in, though it was too late. The headache that formed was a gentle reminder of why he normally avoided drinking. But every once in a while, he needed to leave himself. To forget for a moment that his biological family was all gone. To avoid the truth of it all. The world of intoxication was his chance to leave the reality and float among the clouds.

The dorm was empty once again. He lay down on his bed, staring mindlessly to the ceiling, letting sleep take over his body.

Brandon found himself in the middle of the field once again at dusk. The trees were becoming one unending shadow in the dying light. He saw the structure in the distance and tried to take his first step towards it. He began to walk this time and was able to move his feet through the field, though it felt like he was wading through the ocean, the force of the rough waters trying to hold him back. His legs felt heavy and he was unable to move any faster. His breathing became labored as he slowly made his way toward the edge of the field. But his determination drove his body to push forward, no matter how long it would take.

As he inched closer, the structure became clearer to him. He made out a silver metal roof on what appeared to be a shed. He stopped to rest for a moment, seemingly out of breath, as if he had just run a full marathon. He looked around him and noticed he had barely moved from his original spot, though his heavy breathing and pounding heart told him otherwise.

After what seemed like an eternity, he got close enough to make out details of the shed. Dark wood panels and faded mint green door. Flanking the worn door were a pair of small picture windows with matching, faded mint green trim. The wood around the bottom perimeter appeared to be rotted in spots. There was a small hole in one of the picture windows, the size of a rock, as if someone had once thrown a small stone through it.

The air around him was eerily still, the trees of the forest not stirring, but he suddenly felt as if he was no longer alone.

The hair on his neck and arms began to raise, and he felt tingles along every inch of his back, like something had lightly caressed his spine.

He closed his eyes tight. Something was amiss, and he needed to wake up. *Come on! Wake up!*

He opened them back up to find himself in the same spot, unable to rouse himself from this dream. His heart raced with fear. He considered turning around and going back to the middle of the field, but curiosity pulled him back toward the shed, like a rope attached to his body trying to reel him in. Begrudgingly, he gave in despite his intuition.

He cautiously approached the shed to peer into the broken window and was slightly disappointed with its contents. A rusted shovel leaned up against one corner. In the middle of the room, a worn wooden table that looked like an old desk or small dining table stood by itself on a woven rug. Abandoned cobwebs carelessly hung in every corner, and nothing appeared to be disturbed. He wondered if this shed had been here since he began having these dreams and he just never noticed its presence.

He looked to the front door and saw an old padlock attached to it. He moved himself in front of the door and reached up, carefully sweeping his fingers across the top of the doorjamb.

His fingers stopped at the cool metal of the shed key.

He brushed off the dirt and dust of the old key on the front of his coat, taking a moment to look at it in his hand before inserting it into the padlock. He turned the key and heard the familiar *click* before he released the locking mechanism and carefully pushed the door open.

Standing at the mouth of the door, he closed his eyes briefly, took a deep breath, and exhaled before taking a step inside.

He looked around at the lifeless shed, but there was nothing other than the shovel, rug, and table. He stood wondering if there was something he has missed along the way or what significance this, or any other part of his dream, may have. This shed and this dream suddenly become as foreign to him as a planet in space.

Frustrated, he headed back outside, turning to close the door behind him, before starting back toward the field. He wished he could return to the normal dream, but was this really normal? He wasn't certain of anything anymore. This dream. His life. There were no answers, only more questions.

He stopped just a few feet from the shed one more time, canvassing the world around him, inhaling the damp air and dank smell of wet moss. Suddenly, a cold and brisk breeze rushed past him, moving the hair on his head and sending his heart into overdrive.

He wasn't alone. Someone was here watching his every move.

He slowly turned back to look at the shed and saw someone retract quickly back from the window.

Brandon jumped back instinctively and turned to run.

Chapter Four

Brandon abruptly sat up in his bed, grabbing his chest, trying to suppress the fear inside him. His entire body was drenched in sweat and his head pounded like a timpani drum.

He surveyed the room, his breathing still heavy, his mouth dry with a lingering taste of stale whiskey from the party earlier.

Flipping the switch on the small table lamp, he reached into the top drawer of his bedside table to pop out a couple of ibuprofen from his small pharmaceutical stash. He grabbed the bottle of water next to the lamp and downed them both in record time.

After a few moments, his breath slowed, and he mumbled, "What the fuck?"

He glanced down at the alarm clock. It was 2:17 a.m. He snagged the marbled black and white notebook and a pencil from the nightstand table and began jotting down all that he could remember about his recent dream. The details of the shed's appearance, the table, shovel, and rug. The green tinted sky littered with billowing storm clouds, something that he had never encountered before. The odd breeze that rushed past him before he turned back to the shed. And the person. He or she retracted so quickly that he couldn't make out any defining characteristics.

After finishing what details he could remember, he closed the book and picked up the small, old red tin at the back of his drawer. It was one of the few belongings he kept from the farm. In it, he kept a couple of pictures and a gold crucifix that belonged to his mother. Jimmy had found it in his room the night after his mother disappeared and had given it to him when they moved to Pennsylvania. He rarely wore it, worried he would lose it, but tonight he thought of it and his parents, accepting the ache in his heart instead of ignoring it.

He clutched the cross in his palm and silently sobbed. Shutting the light off and lying back down in his bed, he cried himself back to sleep.

A few hours later, Brandon abruptly woke from his sleep, this time, to the *bring-bring* of his cell phone lying next to him on the pillow.

"Hello?" Brandon muttered, forcing himself to open his eyes fully.

"Hey, Bran!" Brandon recognized his stepdad's deep voice on the other end of the line.

Nervous, he quickly rolled over to check the time, wondering if he had slept late. 7:59 a.m.

"Hi, Dad," he sighed, smiling to himself, his body

melting and relaxing back into the bed. "I guess you don't sleep in on the weekend?"

Jimmy laughed. "I missed you and hadn't heard from you in a few weeks. I thought I'd call to check on you and see if you plan to come down for Thanksgiving?"

A slight tinge of guilt tugged at his heart. He hadn't called Jimmy as often as he should, but he'd been so busy with school. "Yeah, I was thinking I may drive down with Maddie for Thanksgiving week. Anything special planned?"

"Nothing special. It'll probably just be us again, kiddo." Jimmy wasn't much for hosting guests during the holidays, but he never questioned having Maddie over.

He was just as much a father to her as he had been to Brandon since the day they found out about her troubled home life. Brandon remembered how shocking it was to learn her truth.

It had been spring of their junior year and school was almost done for the year. The excitement for summer break to start and the anxiety over final exams in the air was palpable. On the Monday morning of their final week, Maddie hadn't shown up on the bus for school, which wasn't normal for her. She rarely got sick, and even if she battled a cold, she insisted on coming to school when other kids would have begged to stay home. Brandon sat in school that day, watching the time slowly tick by, hoping she would show up late.

She never did.

He rode the bus and got off at her stop instead of his own. As he approached her house, he could see her windows were covered with sheets instead of curtains. The grass looked unruly and trash bags were piled up in the driveway at the side of the house. There was an old, worn, green leather couch that sat on the front porch of the old Bungalow home. He ran up the steps and knocked on the door, worried she may be gone forever, a feeling he was all too familiar with. Maddie answered the door, her cheeks stained with dried mascara from her tears.

"I didn't want you to see me like this, Brandon. I didn't want you to know, but I can't hide this anymore," she had said, throwing herself into his embrace. Brandon held her for a moment, and then with his arm around her shoulders, they walked over and sat together on the worn, green couch, her head resting on his chest. What she said next rocked him to his core. Her mother was an alcoholic and paid little attention to Maddie. Her father left when she was born. Maddie learned early on how to take care of herself, even if it meant lying on applications to get herself into private schools.

He remembered her saying at that moment, "I just want to be normal, Brandon. I wanted to pretend I'm someone I'm not so that I can lead the life that I always dreamed of."

Maddie went on to describe what had happened the night prior. Her mother had gone on a binge, depressed from her latest love disaster, but instead of passing out, she became violently ill and feverish with alcohol poisoning. Maddie had called 9-1-1 to come and pick her mother up, while Maddie stayed behind to clean up the vomit and blood that covered the bathroom floor, too mortified to face school or her friends.

Brandon couldn't leave her like that, in that house full of bad memories and void of love. He brought her home with him that afternoon and told Jimmy about what had happened. She came to live with them, unbeknownst to the school or anyone else, happy to take up the empty third bedroom next to Brandon's.

A week after the incident, Maddie's mother had called Jimmy looking for Maddie so that she could ask her for money. She claimed she needed the money to keep the lights on, but Maddie knew better than this. She didn't ask for her to come home or apologize for what had happened. It was as if she was oblivious to reality, drunk with her self-ishness. Maddie never saw her mother again. Brandon never understood why her mom bothered to check in once in a while when she seemed to care so little for her own daughter.

"You still there?" Jimmy said, interrupting Brandon's thoughts.

"Yeah, sorry, Dad," Brandon replied, sitting himself up in the bed as he brought himself back to the present. He gave Jimmy the schedule for that week so Jimmy could prepare for their arrival.

"Can't wait to see you two!" Jimmy said before hanging up.

Chapter Five

fter battling several hours with his hangover, Brandon decided to meet up with Maddie again at The Constant Brew. He took his seat in the usual spot in the corner across from Maddie, who was surprisingly early for a change. He placed the marbled composition book in front of her and invited her to read his latest entry.

"What is your gut telling you about who this person is, Bran?" she asked after a few moments of reading.

"I know this may sound crazy, but I think it's one of my parents. I didn't really get a good look at the person, but I woke up thinking of them, and that usually doesn't happen," he said, unconsciously rubbing the etchings on the crucifix around his neck. He had placed the necklace around his neck when he got up that morning. The necklace that had been tucked away for a few years, he had decided to bring out of the box and into the light. Today, he could feel her with him.

Maddie took a sip of her coffee and thought for a

moment. "Well, I guess it could be your dad, but didn't you tell me your mom just left? She didn't die, Bran, isn't that what you told me?"

"Nah...that's only what Jimmy believes, but I know deep down that something happened to her and that she has been dead for a long time." Sitting back in his chair, Brandon looked away from Maddie and into the distance, fighting the lump in his throat and the urge to cry again. What if this person in the dream was her? Why did he run from her? He suddenly felt foolish for doing so, worried he wouldn't be able to return to that spot in his dream.

"Brandon?" Maddie began waving her hand in front of his face to grab his attention again, "Are you okay?"

"Sorry, Maddie," he said turning his attention back to her, "I just haven't been able to get my mind off her lately." He sat back up in his chair and looked directly into Maddie's eyes, summoning all his energy to focus on the moment. Inhaling a sharp breath, he continued, "Anyway, are you coming with me back to Dad's house for Thanksgiving?" he asked, ready to move on from the conversation to something else. Brandon needed time alone to sort through his thoughts on his own first.

"Hmmm...let me see," she replied, placing a finger under her chin and looking upward, pretending to ponder the question at length—he knew it was a given, but he loved to invite her just the same. "Hang out here by myself or come home with my bestie? Tough choice!" she said jokingly.

Brandon's phone began to vibrate in his pocket. He reached in and pulled it out. It was a text from Jimmy.

Jimmy: *Hey, buddy, something's come up and we have an unexpected change of plans. Gonna need you to meet up at the farm in Greenville for Thanksgiving week instead of coming back to KOP. I have some business to attend to and you'll need to be there.*
Bran: *Sure, all okay?*
Jimmy: *Yeah, all is fine. I'll tell you more when you get here next week. Nothing to worry about. Can't wait to see you and Maddie May!*

Brandon sat for a moment, stunned and looking like a deer caught in the headlights. He put the phone face down on the table and looked up at Maddie.

"Something is up. That was Jimmy asking me to come back to Greenville for Thanksgiving. He said he has business to talk to me about."

"Um...okay," she said, taking another sip of her latte. "But I can still come with you, right?" she questioned nervously. She wasn't prepared to spend a holiday without him, and she didn't want to miss seeing the farm that Brandon mentioned from time to time.

Brandon quickly relaxed his expression into a smile, not wanting her to worry, though even his own stomach felt as though it were tied in knots.

"Of course! You think I'd leave you here alone on Thanksgiving to have all the fun without me? Nah, I want you to come and spend another miserable holiday with me," he teased. Their holidays together were always fun, even if it was just the three of them.

Brandon wondered what "business" Jimmy needed to discuss with him, as he sat with Maddie talking about their upcoming physics exam, comparing notes and quizzing each other. He had not been to Greenville since he was eight, and the last real memory he had was of his Grandma Alice's funeral. A dark and rainy day, one that was etched in his mind forever. He had watched in tears as they lowered her shiny, cherrywood casket into the cold ground, amidst the other headstones and dead grass. The next few months he lived in a thick fog, vaguely aware of what was going on around him. He could only eat, sleep, and go to school. He didn't want to play soccer or hang out with his friends; it just didn't feel right anymore with her gone. She had made living at the farm so special despite losing his parents so early on. And then when Jimmy announced at the end of that same school year that they needed to pack up and move to start over, Brandon had felt the same heartache he felt when he learned of his grandma's passing. The kind of loss that seemed to rob him of his breath and left him paralyzed, unable to protest. They packed a few belongings into the bed of Jimmy's F-150, grabbed Bella, his loyal companion, and set off for a new life. Jimmy never looked back, but Brandon couldn't keep his eyes off the farm as they rolled down the long driveway.

As much sorrow as he had felt for the months that followed that day when they left that farm, he had learned to appreciate where he was now. Not all were lucky enough to find such a friendship in life like the one he had with Maddie, their bond sealed by fate.

Brandon raised his hand to get the attention of the server to bring their check. As they began to pack up to head back to the dorms for the night, he felt a small hint of excitement for their upcoming trip through all the nervousness and anxiety. He wanted to share all of his fondest memories of the farm with her, to show her the fields where he learned to play soccer, the secret closets tucked away in the old house, and the trails he used to ride horses on. This was also his chance to learn more about what happened to his mother. Small towns never forget, and he was bound to find someone who knew something. Perhaps he could piece together what they had missed two decades before.

Chapter Six

Back in his dorm room, Brandon began packing his belongings for the long week ahead. As he carefully arranged the clothes in his bag, he let all the memories of his life at the farm flood his mind like a dam giving way to the water it held back in its protective walls. He wondered why Jimmy stopped taking him there after they had moved to King of Prussia. He knew that the long-time caretaker, Evan Holt, had stayed behind to take care of the property, but he never heard from him, and Brandon hoped that he kept up the farm the way his grandmother would have liked it.

He zipped up his duffel bag and placed it by the door for the next morning. He sat back down on the edge of his bed, taking the red tin box out of the nightstand once again, pulling the picture of his parents out. He cradled it with his hands in his lap and examined every inch of the glossy paper. It was the only picture he had of them together, and he kept it sealed away, protecting it like a mother protecting her cub, careful not to expose it to the harsh realities of the world.

He brushed his thumb over his mother's cheek, a beautiful woman with black curly hair and tanned skin. His father was tall and athletic with a kind-looking face and the same eyes that Brandon inherited, as green as the sea. They were sitting in the back of his grandparents' old Ford truck, a classic black antique from the 50s. Zach and Ella were smiling at each other as if one had told a joke to the other, the summer sun setting behind them in a field of golden wheat and weeping willow trees. Brandon could feel the love they had for each other through his picture, the two of them seemingly at peace and living in the moment. He hoped he would have a love as strong as theirs someday. He kissed the picture and walked it over to the bag he had packed, putting it in the front pocket to carry with him on his journey.

Brandon looked back at the clock; it was just after ten in the evening, and he wanted to get to bed at a decent time, knowing they had a long drive ahead. He turned off his bedside light and lay stretched out on his bed, his hands behind his head, staring at the popcorn ceiling. His only thought at that moment was that of his parents and the farm, wondering what they would be doing if they were still alive. As he drifted off to sleep, he couldn't help but wish it was them that he was bringing Maddie home to see.

Brandon found himself in the field, surrounded by the familiar wheat again. The sky was covered in a smooth blanket of storm clouds, and sparks of lightning pierced the ground in the far distance. The wind picked up and the trees began to sway angrily back and forth, the leaves from the ground swirling around in the air, like a mini tornado that just formed. He felt the first droplet of rain on his cheek. He began to walk toward the shed, and the sky opened up to a heavy rain, almost torrential.

Running in the rain to the front of the shed, he stopped just a few feet from the door, holding his arm up as a shield from the thick droplets of water as he looked around. He could see the goosebumps on his arms and the tingle of anxiety down his spine. He knew he was being watched from the woods. Slowly, he turned his head to look through the woods, but all he could see were the bare trees, their leaves in a pile of mush covering the ground soaked with rain. The shadows in the distance seemed to be playing tricks on his mind. It was too hard to make out anything with the heavy rain, so he turned his attention back to the shed. As his eyes made their way to the window on the left, he saw her.

A woman!

His heart started galloping like a horse through the open plains. She stared at him through the other side of the glass.

The door of the shed forced itself open with the storm winds and hit the side of the shed with a loud WHACK! Brandon jumped back and gasped. Suddenly, the rain let up just enough so he could make out the details of the woman who was still standing behind the glass, her face stoic and unfazed by the storm going on outside.

His breath became labored and his heart beat so loud he was certain she could hear it too. He stood there frozen with his eyes locked on hers, afraid that if he moved, the woman would disappear. Her eyes were as dark as coals, her tanned skin was streaked with dirt, her disheveled hair held loosely in place with a band on top of her head.

Her throat! He noticed a deep gash that spanned across the middle, fresh with blood that stained her white shirt.

He slowly walked toward the window, his eyes never leaving hers. Her eyes widened and her facial expression began to morph as if she were the one seeing the ghost.

He studied her face, unable to think about who she was but knowing she felt familiar to him. *Think, dammit!* Brandon worried his dream would end at any moment and he would never figure out who this woman was.

She moved her right hand to place her dirt-covered palm against the glass. A tear began to form in her eye, soon welling over and spilling down her cheek, leaving a clean path in its wake. He placed his palm on the other side of the pane on top of hers, the two of them staring at each other for what seemed like an eternity as he studied her every feature.

And then it suddenly hit him like the lightning bolt that tore through the sky above him. He knew this woman.

"Mom?"

Chapter Seven

Brandon quickly sat up on his bed, his breath labored, ripped from his dream like someone pulled him out from a burning fire. He glanced at his clock; it was almost seven in the morning. He looked around his room, trying to ground himself in reality again. His eyes stopped at the bag he had packed by the door, remembering the picture of his parents he put in the front pocket. Thinking this may have sparked his latest dream, he dismissed it as a coincidence, unable to admit to himself that it had any significance. There was no way that could be his mom. These types of dreams happened all the time, he thought to himself. He raked his fingers through his curly hair and put his dream behind him as he got out of bed and walked to the bathroom to get himself ready for the trip.

He stood at the mirror and picked up his phone to text Maddie, making sure she was awake and would be ready to go in thirty minutes. As he brushed his teeth, he couldn't help but think about his dream, despite trying to push it to the back corners of his mind. *I'm losing my fucking mind.*

There is no way Mom is trying to communicate with me through a fucking dream. Get real, Bran, he thought to himself. He dismissed the thoughts and thrust the feelings of anxiety back down to his gut. He was nervous enough about returning to the farm and didn't need this added complexity in his life right now. Letting out a low laugh, he shook his head back and forth, rolling his eyes at himself. *Get a grip on yourself! It's just a goddamned dream!*

He finished getting ready and took one last minute to look around his room, making sure he hadn't left anything. Convinced he had what he needed, he grabbed his leather jacket and the packed duffel bag and headed out the door.

He walked out of the building, and clear skies and plenty of sunshine greeted him. It was cool, but not so cold that he could see pillows of his own breath wafting in the air. He walked to the back lot to the black Jeep Wrangler that he had just purchased a few months prior. Brandon was not one to splurge all the time, but after driving around an old beater since high school—a real clunker referred to as Rusty—he decided that it was time to treat himself a little. He threw his duffel in the trunk, got behind the steering wheel, and turned the key. The engine roared to life. He mindlessly flipped through channels on the radio to find something decent to listen to as he waited for Maddie.

After a few minutes, he saw her approaching from the distance. Her hair was pulled back, and she was bundled in a black peacoat, jeans, and a cream-colored scarf carefully draped around her neck. He was in awe of her beauty. She was the type of girl who could throw anything on and look stunning, but today she looked ravishing. He smiled and waved to her through the window. He loved Maddie, but he tried not to think of her romantically, at least that's what he convinced himself. Their friends would tease them from time to time, asking why they wouldn't just hook up and get on with it. But Brandon would laugh it off. She was his best friend, after all. He never asked her if the rumors ever offended her or even if she was interested in him. He was afraid to know the truth and let her in to his life fully. It was a small price to pay to avoid the pain of losing someone he cared for so deeply. A pain he knew all too well.

She opened the trunk and placed her suitcase and purse next to his bags before settling into the passenger seat next to Brandon. "Hey, Bran!" she said, smiling and reaching in for a hug. Brandon breathed in the scent of her perfume.

"Morning, Maddie May," he said, knowing full well she hated getting called that name from anyone other than Jimmy. She rolled her eyes at him and smiled back.

He pulled out of the parking space and headed down the street to The Constant Brew to get coffee for the trip ahead. He parked the car on the street in front of the doors and walked in to get them coffee, leaving Maddie in the car to stay warm.

As Brandon stood at the counter inside, waiting for the barista to finish frothing the milk for Maddie's latte, he allowed his mind to wonder on whatever thoughts seemed most prominent. The memory of his mother kept returning to the front of his mind like a revolving door that he could not get out of. He couldn't help but wonder what life would be like now with her here. What may have happened the last night he remembered seeing her. What if she would have never met Jimmy...?

The cashier collected his money and handed him two

hot coffees in return. He headed back out to the truck, handed Maddie the drinks, and blurted out, "I need to find out what happened to my mom."

"Geez, Bran, must we start the day on such a serious note? I haven't even had my first sip yet," Maddie said jokingly.

"I'm serious!" Brandon replied, getting behind the wheel again. "I had another one of those dreams last night, Maddie. But this time, there was a woman in it, and she was alive but also dead, with a gaping wound across her neck. I think she's trying to tell me something."

"Okay, okay, I get it. You know I'm joking. Give me the highlight reel," she replied, slowly taking a sip of her latte.

As Brandon pulled out of his parking space and headed for I-84 east toward New York, he shared with her all of the detail he could remember. She sat in the passenger seat, mostly in silence, but acknowledging him from time to time, letting him know she was listening. It was a gorgeous fall day. The peak for fall foliage had ended and the sea of red and gold-colored leaves covering the landscape around them had already faded to grays and browns. It was still just as beautiful, Brandon thought. The sun was bright and warmed their faces through the truck. It was hard to believe that a storm would be coming in just a few days.

Brandon filled her in on the latest dream as Maddie listened in silence to every detail.

"It sounds like your dream is getting more and more intense each night. Do you think it has anything to do with the fact that we are going back to the farm and your mind is overthinking what happened?"

Brandon shrugged his shoulders and immediately

changed the subject. "Did I ever tell you about the time I broke my arm falling out of the tree by the lake up there?"

"No! When did this happen?"

"It's a funny story actually. I was four years old and fell deep in love with Riley, the girl my grandma sometimes had come to watch me. The day I met her, I got so scared that I ran out of the house and up the tree as I usually did. Buutttt, I could not miss out on what she was saying so I dangled as low as I could to try and listen in on their conversation. I fell out of the tree and broke my damn arm." He laughed at the memory though he remembered crying for hours the day it happened.

"Do you ever reach out to Riley?"

"No. She left for college not long before I moved to the city."

Brandon couldn't believe how long it had been since he last saw the farm, and in just a few hours, he would be back at the place that brought him so much happiness as a child. He continued to share his memories of the farm with Maddie, leaving talk of his mom's sudden disappearance theory in the rearview mirror for the moment.

His Grandma Alice had let Jimmy stay on after Brandon's parents had passed away. She didn't want her grandson to be so far from her, and that was fine by Brandon.

There were three houses on the sprawling property. The guest house at the front entrance where Evan stayed, the main house where his grandmother lived, and next to that was the little cabin where Brandon lived. Brandon would go over each morning to have breakfast in Alice's kitchen. She would be busy making pancakes or eggs, always wearing a dress and an embroidered apron around her waist. He would try to sneak up on her, but she always sensed his presence before he could ever try scaring her. He would run up into her open arms and give her a hug. She called him her little angel.

She would sit and tell him stories about his parents, stories he cherished. When they weren't talking, Brandon would spend his days helping around the farm here and there. He especially loved to wander around the woods, exploring with his friends or his dog, Bella. Brandon grew up dreaming of finding his mom so he could bring her back and share his adventures with her. Some days he felt the truth in his soul, and it brought him great pain, while other days he ignored the truth in favor of happiness and peace. It was easier to live in fantasy anyway.

But those dreams came to a sudden halt just after his eighth birthday when Alice became ill with cancer. Instead of being greeted in the kitchen for breakfast each morning, Brandon would go up to her room, sit next to her bedside, and watch her try to hide the pain she was feeling. A few short months after learning she was sick, she slipped away into sleep and never opened her eyes again. It was after that moment that Brandon realized that she was not coming back. She was gone forever, just like his mother and father.

Silence took over the space for a few moments after Brandon finished sharing his story with Maddie.

"I'm sorry about your family, Brandon," Maddie said, surprised that he had opened up so much to her. She had asked him questions about his past from time to time, but he had always seemed reluctant to share.

"It's okay, Maddie. I try not to let it get the best of me,

ya know? I just picked up the pieces, sealed them away, and moved on," he replied. He knew that was only partly true, though. He could never seal them away forever. During his time away from the farm and the period where Maddie lived with him, Brandon had been unable to open himself up to sharing everything with her until now. The family history wasn't pretty, but then again, who had a picture-perfect past? He could only write the now and the future to come.

They crossed the state line from Pennsylvania into New York, and just as they approached exit 2 to Mountain Road from the interstate, a strange uneasiness filled his stomach. It turned in knots like someone was kneading a ball of dough, and his head had a dull ache. The anxiety he began to feel was overwhelming coming back to this small town. He didn't anticipate that this would wreak havoc on his psyche so quickly, but he knew this time, he needed to find and accept the truth.

Chapter Eight

Brandon and Maddie arrived ahead of schedule, and Jimmy wasn't expecting them until after 2 p.m. He encouraged them to explore the town before heading to the farm so he had time to get there and greet them.

"Jimmy isn't here yet," Brandon said, placing his phone in the console area. "Do you want to get something to eat before we head over? I'm sure we can find something around here."

"Yeah," Maddie replied sarcastically, looking around at vast farmland surrounding them, "it looks like a real swanky town, Bran. I'm sure the restaurants are plentiful."

As they headed west on the main stretch of town, Brandon could see that Maddie was right. He didn't remember the town being so desolate when he was younger. There was nothing for miles except for a farmhouse tucked away from the road here and there. Rustic farmhouses that seemed well kept and horses that roamed the fields around them. Up ahead, Brandon spotted a red building with a sign that said "Vinny's" in front. It looked like a house more than a restaurant, with white trim and a black tin roof. He pulled into the empty parking lot in front of the flashing "open" sign that appeared in the window.

They stepped inside the main entrance and stood next to the empty hostess stand. The floors were white linoleum like a school lunchroom, the ceiling was low and covered with tin tiles, the windows adorned with antique-looking window treatments, and Christmas lights hung around the perimeter of the one-room restaurant. A lady behind the bar at the far end of the restaurant had her back to them but could see them come in from the reflection in the mirror behind the array of spirits that lined the back of the bar. She appeared to be on the phone but motioned them in to come and sit down.

Brandon and Maddie walked over and placed their jackets on the coat rack next to the bar and then took seats at the end, waiting for the server to finish her call. There were no more than a dozen tables in the empty dining space behind them, all covered with cheap red and white checked tile and a small votive candle in the center. Despite the outdated and eclectic décor, it had a cozy feel, and Brandon imagined that the local folks probably enjoyed having a place to come and hang out in this quiet town.

The bartender finished her call and grabbed a couple of water glasses before turning around to head over to where they sat. As she approached them, her smile faded on her round face, and she stopped in her tracks. The glasses she held came crashing down as she threw her hands to her mouth and gasped.

Brandon and Maddie quickly looked at each other,

perplexed by the bartender's reaction, before Brandon stood up to walk around the bar.

"Are you okay, ma'am?" Brandon asked. She looked as if she had just seen a ghost.

She slowly removed her chubby hands from her mouth, her smile returning to her round face. She was a beautiful woman, short and plump, with cropped dark brown hair and dark eyes. "I...I'm so sorry! Please, don't worry about me. Have a seat and let me get this mess cleaned," she said, running to retrieve the broom and dustpan in the corner. "I'll get your order here in just a sec!"

Once she was done cleaning up the glass and returning the broom to the corner, she returned. "Now!" She smiled and breathed an exaggerated sigh of relief in fun. "What can I get for you two?" Her eyes never left Brandon's face.

"We'll just take two waters, please," Maddie asked, trying to hand her back the menus. "Are you sure you're okay?"

"Sure, water, no problem," she acknowledged Maddie without ever looking her in the eye; her own baggy eyes were seemingly under a spell. She turned halfway, never noticing that Maddie was attempting to hand her something, and then turned back, "I'm sorry, but I have to ask. I know just about everyone around here, but I have not seen you two in here before, but you look so familiar. Are you visiting family?" she pried.

"Oh...uh...yes, but this is my first time back in almost thirteen years. My name is Brandon Stone, and my family owns Stone Farm up the road," he replied, holding his hand out to introduce himself. "Have you heard of it?"

"Heard of it! Of course! Now I know where I recognize

you! You must be Zach and Ella's son!" she said excitedly as she made the connection. "Forgive me, my name is Violet Castillo. I've lived in this town my whole life, so I'm what they call the town historian," she said and giggled, as proud of her title as a child receiving ice cream.

Brandon introduced Maddie, and Violet shook her hand with a friendly smile before diverting her attention back to Brandon with a more serious face. "I'm very sorry about your father. And your mother? I couldn't believe my ears when I heard she disappeared. Did you ever find out what happened to her?"

Nosey was more like it, Brandon thought of Violet. No wonder they called her the historian. "Did you know my parents?" He hesitated before answering her questions.

"Yes, of course. We all went to school together, and I happened to be in the same grade."

"Well, to answer your question, I don't know what happened to my mother. I was sort of looking to learn more about what happened that night while I'm here with Maddie—and my stepdad, Jimmy Callahan."

"Jimmy!" she shrieked. "I haven't seen him since he left here thirteen years ago!"

Violet explained to them how she had been friends with Zach, Ella, and Jimmy while in high school. More like acquaintances, really; the three were so close that there wasn't much room for anyone else. But they were friendly with everyone. She remembered the day that Ella had disappeared. It felt as though it were just yesterday. Nothing had ever shaken this town in that way before. It was like an earthquake had rocked the town so badly that it left a hole in the center of its heart. Greenville was just like any other small town: it had many good people, and tragedies were just unheard of.

The police investigated and interviewed everyone in town. Search parties were formed, and every inch of the town was turned over. They found nothing. Not a single stitch of evidence. It was like she was just abducted by aliens, and they left no trace behind. The town was divided about what truly happened. Some thought she may have been murdered, but there were some who assumed she just ran away.

It was no secret that she was unhappy in her new marriage, spending many a night at the bar just to get out of the house. Some suspected she was having an affair with a local named Chad. The two had become very friendly at the bar, but Violet knew better than that. She could tell when a woman was only seeking companionship and not love. Chad, on the other hand, seemed to be head over heels for her. He still lived in town, but after Ella disappeared, he stopped coming into the bar. Police had no reason to believe he had anything to do with her disappearance. Supposedly, his alibi was rock solid.

Violet mindlessly cleaned the bar with a rag, focused on a spot where someone's sauce had dried up earlier as she finished recalling every detail she could think of. "I had plenty of theories, but no one cared to listen." She sighed an audible sigh. "Anyway, I hope you two enjoy your lunch. I'm here if you need me."

"Thank you for sharing that. It was helpful," he said.

"Anytime," Violet replied over her shoulder as she retreated back to the kitchen, balancing cups she had stacked about a foot high between her hands.

Brandon looked back to Maddie and mouthed "wow" to her with his lips.

"Yep. Looks like we have a lot to unpack here," Maddie acknowledged. The two turned to the food in front of them and ate.

As Brandon and Maddie finished up their lunch, Violet emerged from behind the curtain to the kitchen to collect their dishes and drop the check. She looked at Brandon and said, "Listen, I can't imagine what it must have been like for you growing up without your parents. I'm not sure what more you will learn in this town, but I've always suspected murder, I don't care what the police said. Call it a hunch. I never suspected Chad, but he may be able to answer questions for you. He was head over heels for your mama, that I know."

She slipped him a piece of paper that had Chad's name on it with an address and wished them luck before disappearing into the kitchen again without saying another word.

Chapter Nine

Brandon thought of the piece of paper with Chad's address that he had shoved in his pocket on their drive to the farm. He wondered if Violet's intuition held any merit. She seemed so certain of her theory of Chad's involvement in his mother's disappearance. He knew he had to pay Chad a visit to get his side of the story. He needed to hear it directly from the source.

As they turned off the main highway onto Overland Drive toward the farm, Brandon's headache returned in full force, like a punch to the temple. He winced in pain at the unexpected force and pulled the Jeep over to the side of the road.

"Are you okay, Bran?"

He massaged his temples and closed his eyes as he tried to get control of the pain. "Yeah, I'll be okay," he lied as the pain grew stronger. His stomach suddenly felt like a pile of mush that was being turned with a mixer. He quickly got out of the car for air, leaning against the Jeep for support.

Maddie got out with him and stood by, rubbing his back in silence, waiting for him to recover.

Overland Drive was a long, windy lane that led directly to the family's private road. Trees flanked both sides, forming a canopy above the road. Brandon looked around to the vast forest filled with naked trees. Hints of green peeked through from the pine trees that stood in between the oak and maple. No other signs of life here, just land and trees.

Brandon's headache subsided after standing there silently with her for a couple of minutes. "Sorry, Maddie! I don't know what just happened," he said, feeling slightly embarrassed at his sudden ailment. "I don't know where that came from."

"It's okay, Bran. It's probably just anxiety. Let me take it from here," she said, sliding into the driver's seat, giving him no time to protest. "I think I can handle the GPS instructions for a couple of miles." She winked at him before pulling the door closed in an effort to help him relax a bit.

A few minutes later, they came to the mouth of Stone Drive. The entrance was beautiful, flanked with large stones on either side of the gravel road. An ornate iron sign etched with the family name greeted them. They passed the small white cottage where Evan stayed, tucked back from the road just past the entrance. Another mile through thick trees on the single-lane road and they reached a clearing. It was as if they had exited reality and entered a separate world. Acres upon acres of soft rolling hills, a pond, and nature fields. The main house was located toward the back of the property, a sprawling old white farmhouse with black shutters, a barnyard red front door, and a wraparound porch. To the left of them was another house, a modest log cabin with its own separate driveway that led to the garage on the side. All of it encompassed in a barrier of trees around all sides.

Brandon instructed Maddie to park in the roundabout in front of the main house. He stepped out of his car to take in the beauty. He had forgotten how much he missed this place. The fields were dormant now with the season, but he could still remember the smell of the sweet grass in the summer and how he would search for wildlife among the Queen Anne's lace and black-eyed Susan found in pockets around the fields. The pond around the back of the house sparkled like flecks of gold in the rays of the sun, and ripples of water danced gently with the cool, fall breeze. He was finally home.

"Brandon?"

Startled by a strange voice, Brandon turned around to see a man walking toward them—tall, with short gray hair and a matching beard. He was as tall as Brandon, dressed in a buffalo plaid flannel, work pants, and worn brown leather working boots.

"I didn't mean to startle you and your lady friend," he said, reaching out his hand to greet them. "Not sure if you recognize me, son, but I'm Evan Holt. I'm still living in the old cottage you passed on the way up the driveway."

Brandon smiled and shook his hand in return before introducing Maddie to him. It had been thirteen years since he had last seen Evan, and he seemed so much smaller to him now. His face was heavy with wrinkles like a Shar Pei and his hands as rough as sandpaper from the winters spent working the farm. Evan never spoke much to him as a child, but Brandon loved to follow him around like a lost puppy, intrigued by whatever work he saw him doing at the farm, a cloud of smoke from his cigarettes surrounding him like an orb.

"I almost didn't recognize you, Mr. Holt," Brandon said.

"Please, call me Evan," he said, his face remaining stoic. "I probably had less gray hair back then. Jimmy called my house just a bit ago and should be here within the hour. He said to take your pick on the houses. The main house is all ready to go, and your parents' old house is also open," he said, pointing toward the mid-sized cabin just off to their left. "I wasn't sure where you'd feel most comfortable."

Brandon suddenly felt an emptiness wash over him as he looked at the last house he had lived in here at the farm. "We'll stay in Mom's old house," he replied without hesitation.

Maddie placed her hand on his shoulder and turned to him slightly. She whispered in his ear just enough so that Evan would not hear. "You sure you feel comfortable staying there, Bran?"

Brandon placed a hand over hers and gave her a reassuring smile.

He wanted to submerge himself into the ocean of both the joy and pain. He wanted to unlock whatever memories he had stored in his psyche in hopes that he could pick up some clues about his mother.

Evan handed them the key, nodded his head in a goodbye, and turned around to walk back toward his own cabin.

Maddie and Brandon moved the Jeep to the driveway leading up to his parents' cabin. They pulled the bags out of the trunk and walked up the paved sidewalk to the covered front porch. The outside was immaculate. Gutters and sidewalks were cleared of any leaves, and there were no weeds in the flowerbeds in front of the porch. Brandon was glad that Evan had put so much care into the property over the years, not allowing time and neglect to infect the natural beauty of it all.

Brandon slid the key in the door and unlocked it before slowly opening it. He stepped inside with Maddie just behind him and stood in the entranceway, taking in everything he could with his eyes. Everything was just the same as he had remembered. The front door opened up to the living room, where the large stone fireplace with a small potbelly stove still stood. To the right of them was a dining area with an adjacent open kitchen. The air was clean and smelled of pine from the logs that made up the exterior walls, and the lights in the house gave it a warm glow, like the embers in a dying fire.

"Let's settle in to the bedrooms and then we can figure out what to do next," Brandon said as he led her to the first bedroom to the left of the living room.

His mother's bedroom. He wasn't ready to take it in, so he left Maddie to settle in on her own for a moment while he went to the next room.

He made his way down the small hallway to the second bedroom where he had once slept. He took a deep breath in before opening the door. The twin trundle bed with his sports themed coverings was neatly made and ready for him. The old rocking chair by the window where his mother once held him and rocked him to sleep was still there, along with the many soccer medals and trophies that adorned his dresser. In the opposite corner was his old crib, an antique that his grandmother insisted he leave in the room well after he was done using it. It was used for his own father and then for him. He could remember his mom laying him in there at night after she sang to him, and his heart ached.

"Hey, you okay?" Maddie asked, resting her hand on his back. Brandon didn't realize she had been standing in the doorway behind him.

"Yeah, I'm fine," he said, placing his bag on the floor next to the crib. "This room used to be mine...well, still is, I guess."

She smiled at him and then moved toward him to give him a hug. She couldn't put into words what she thought he needed to hear at that moment.

They walked down past the bathroom that separated two of the bedrooms and into his parents' old master bedroom again. This time Brandon stepped past the threshold and held his breath for a few seconds before taking it all in. It was a larger room with a king-size four-poster bed, matching dresser, and a plush chair for reading in the corner. In the opposite corner was a large, antique armoire used as the primary closet. A sun tube in the ceiling flooded the room with light, giving the room a bright, airy feeling. Next to the window was his mom's old chair with a table next to it, stacked with her old books. It was as if time stood still. Nothing moved. No one wanted to move on from that terrible night.

Brandon's cell phone buzzed, breaking the momentary silence in the room, as he placed the luggage on the luggage rack at the foot of the bed. He pulled the phone out of the pocket to answer it as Maddie stood waiting for his next cue.

"Hey, Dad," he said, smiling at Maddie.

"Hey, bud, I'm here! I saw your Jeep outside the cabin.

I'm up at the main house getting settled. Why don't you and Maddie come on over?"

Brandon agreed and hung up with his stepdad.

"It's showtime!" Brandon teased, throwing his hands up next to his head, showcasing like a performer. Maddie giggled in response. Her laugh was contagious and made Brandon feel more at ease. The laughter continued as they turned and headed back toward the living room to grab their coats and start walking toward the main house.

It was late in the afternoon, and the sun was already beginning to set past the tree line behind the house, the burnt orange glow highlighting the mostly bare trees surrounding the farm.

Jimmy came out on the rocking chair porch, waving and smiling his familiar smile, a coffee mug in his hand. He wore a thick fleece button down shirt and lined jeans, his face freshly shaved. The years had been good to him. His face still appeared young, despite the increase in crow's feet next to his eyes. He still had a full head of dark brown hair, lightly dusted near his sideburns with gray.

"Maddie!" he shouted, as he walked down the steps to greet them with hugs. "I swear you look more and more beautiful each time I see you." He put an arm around Brandon and invited them to come inside out of the cold. "I'm so glad you guys made it safely. It will be nice to spend Thanksgiving up here for the first time in a while," he said, but Brandon knew he was not being completely truthful. Jimmy made it clear when they had moved out that he did not want to return. But he was happy Jimmy was at least trying to make an effort.

They walked inside Grandma Alice's house to the faint

smells of his grandmother's old lavender soap lingering in the air somehow. They stood in the foyer, a formal dining room to the left and a living area to the right. Both rooms had large fireplaces, and Jimmy had taken the liberty of lighting the hearth in the living room. Just down the hall in front of them, beyond the stairs, was the kitchen where Brandon spent most of his time with his grandmother. He could still remember her in her embroidered apron, standing next to him at the stove, explaining what she was doing in hopes that he would someday learn to become a decent chef to his own family. Though Brandon didn't quite pick up all of her culinary skills, he could make a delicious Sunday gravy and was a whiz at flipping omelets in the pan. He made a low chuckle, knowing she would have some silly joke to say about his limitations in the kitchen.

Jimmy led them into the living room and invited them to sit on the couch in front of the warm fireplace. He had a large, caramel-colored envelope tucked under his left arm.

"Brandon, I'm sure there is a part of you wondering why I chose to come back to this farm," he said, standing across from them in front of the fire. He looked at the envelope and traced the letters on the front of it with his thumb. "Dealing with the past just isn't my thing, but I have known that we would need to return here for quite some time," he continued, a sea of sadness washing over his face as he handed the envelope over and asked Brandon to open it.

Brandon took out the contents, revealing the last will of the estate.

"Your grandmother had already handed over the reins for this place to your parents before you were born," he explained.

Brandon's eyes locked on the words on the first page of the large file in his lap, unable to move or speak. Maddie placed her hand on his leg, the heat from her hand radiating through his jeans like a heating blanket warming his blood.

"When your dad passed away, your mom had created a trust to make sure you were taken care of in case anything happened to her. She built in protections to make sure you didn't have access until you were twenty-one. I think she would be at peace knowing you are more than capable of handling yourself and this property, if you're interested in keeping it," Jimmy said, conveying a sense of pride in Brandon's accomplishments.

"That envelope has just about everything you want to know about this land and all that comes with it. I know this is a lot to take..." Jimmy paused briefly before continuing, "Just know that I support you in whatever decision you make. You have a lot going on with school and big plans for your future. Running a farm may not be something you wanna take on, and I get that. I'm sure there'd be plenty of caring folks with interest in this place if you decide to sell it," he continued, trying to reassure Brandon. "Sorry to spring this on you during your week off, but I wanted to get it out of the way first."

If Jimmy felt anger at this moment, Brandon thought he concealed it well. He had a warm smile on his face and Brandon knew this must not be not easy for him. Coming to the farm was like unwrapping the bandage from the old wounds that never healed and the pain was likely overwhelming. Jimmy made it clear from time to time that he did not want to talk about Ella. Anytime Brandon mentioned his mother's name, Jimmy would always change the subject abruptly. He admired Jimmy anyway. He always treated him like he was his biological son, and for that, he was grateful.

Brandon tried to soak in every word Jimmy had said while thumbing through the stack of papers in his lap. He supposed he knew in the back of his mind that this day was coming, but in a way, it still felt like a shock to his nervous system. And though he knew his mom was not coming back, this made it feel so final.

"Anyway, just think about it," Jimmy said, breaking the silence in the room. "In the meantime, let's make the best of this week we have here for Thanksgiving. I need to run to town to get food for the house and I'll be back in a few hours."

He stood up and headed out the front door, placing his hand on Brandon's shoulder for a moment before leaving them there to digest the news.

Brandon took a few moments to sit with Maddie before breaking the silence between them. "Never in a million years did I expect any of this," Brandon said to Maddie, still clinging to the papers. He had been planning to attend med school next year and wasn't sure how he could handle running the farm and finishing school.

"Bran, this could be great, you know? You could get your medical degree closer to home and practice here in town!" Maddie said. She inched in closer to him and put her arm around his back. "Listen, there is a reason for everything, right? Life is about taking the opportunities that are handed to you and running with them, no matter how overwhelming it feels."

Brandon feigned a smile. He wished he could share in

her excitement, but the breadth of what was to come with the farm felt so overwhelming, and a tightness pulled around his chest. He couldn't think of this right now. This was the least of his worries. He needed closure on his mother before he could make any rational decisions about this place. Finding her would help guide his decision on the fate of the farm.

Chapter Ten

After a long day, Brandon crashed early, then woke up feeling rested and ready to explore the town and start fresh. He sat up and rubbed the sleep from his eyes. Violet had mentioned Chad when they arrived in town, and that would be Brandon's first stop before asking Jimmy more questions, knowing he needed more time to settle in at the farm first.

Brandon got out of bed and quickly got ready before he planned to make Maddie and himself coffee and breakfast. He came out of his room to find he was too late. Maddie had already prepared a large breakfast and set up places at the kitchen counter for them to eat.

"Morning!" she said, filled with her usual burst of positive energy. "I hope you don't mind me using the kitchen. I woke up early and needed to keep busy while you got ready."

"You really know your way to my heart, dontcha?" Brandon smiled as she blushed. He sauntered over to the counter and eyed the feast before him of fresh scrambled eggs, toast with butter and bacon cooked to perfection. His mouth watered in anticipation.

The two of them sat down and devoured the breakfast while discussing their action plan for the day. Maybe calling Chad would be a better idea instead of just showing up and confronting him face-to-face, but Brandon was afraid he wouldn't answer or that Chad would hang up before he got his questions out. They decided to drive to his house together to confront the last man known to be seen with Ella.

After cleaning up the dishes, Brandon and Maddie grabbed their coats and headed outside into the cold air. The sun over the horizon made a weak attempt at heating things up. Briskly walking to the Jeep, the two of them got into the vehicle and blasted the heater, sitting in the driveway shivering until warm air finally started to seep through the vents.

The address that Violet had given them the day before was a short, fifteen-minute drive from the farm. They pulled out and began the journey. The drive was quiet, as Brandon's mind was filled was thoughts. He wondered what kind of man Chad was and what he might learn from him about his mother. Maddie, however, seemed content just looking out the window at her surroundings.

"Looks like that's the place." Brandon pointed to a small, gray ranch style house off the main road. The house looked older and in need of some repair. Shingles were curled in various spots on the roof and the paint was peeling away along the siding. Brandon parked behind an old Ford pickup truck in the driveway.

"Brandon, are you sure you want to do this?" Maddie

asked, her brow furrowed as she examined the state of the house.

Brandon knew how Maddie felt about poking around the past. She believed it was better to let the past stay where it was most of the time and just move forward. She was ever the optimist, but for good reason. She had told him that she worried that he would uncover facts about his mother's demise that would alter his feelings and memories of her in a negative way.

"We'll be fine, trust me. I have to do this," he said as he reached for her hand and squeezed it softly.

A few moments later, they stood on the small front stoop at the front of the house. Brandon knocked at the rusted, old storm door. They could hear someone inside walking toward the door, and slowly it began to open. A tall man in a plain white t-shirt and faded jeans opened the door, looking at them both before speaking.

"Can I help you?" he asked, puzzled by the presence of people on his property.

"Uh...hi there. My name is Brandon Stone, and this is my girlfriend, Maddie." He didn't want to explain their relationship, and "girlfriend" seemed like the best title at the moment. "Sorry to just drop in on you like this, but I think you know my mother, Ella Callahan, and I'm wondering if I can ask you a few questions?" Brandon asked, his brow tingling with cold sweat.

"Correction..." he replied curtly. "I *knew* your mother. She's dead, right? Not sure what else I can tell you."

"Listen, I'm sure you've heard that some folks in this town are on the fence about what happened," he said condescendingly. "But I'm a realist. She'd a come back here by now if she were alive and she never did," he continued. A few moments of uncomfortable silence passed before Chad let out an apologetic sigh. "Look...I'm sorry about your mom, kid. I can tell you what I know, but I can't say you're gonna like what I have to say, is all." He moved out of the way to let the two of them inside.

Brandon took Maddie's hand and led them inside the small, ranch house. The inside was not at all what either of them had expected from the looks of the outside. The inside was spotless and almost inviting. The walls were adorned with old family photos. The couches looked cozy. There wasn't a hint of dust on anything from what Brandon could see, and the kitchen, just off the living room, looked fit enough for any small chef, with polished copper pots and pans hanging neatly above the gas stove and a collection of designer knives to the left of it.

Chad took his seat at the antique dining table, round and made of dark cherry wood. He motioned for them to join him. Brandon and Maddie quietly took their seats across the table from him. He watched them carefully as he rubbed the stubble on his beard, thinking of what to say to them first.

"Best not to beat around the bush, I suppose," he said, looking out the window as if looking through a window in time. "I was sweet on your mom for a while. I met her over at Vinny's one night about eight months before she died. I had just moved up here from the city a couple of years before but had never seen her in there. She sure was a sight," he said with a half-smile before turning to look at them.

"I noticed she was wearing a ring, but no man ever came

in with her. One night, I started talking to her, and it was like this instant connection. Eventually, she told me about her marital problems and her plans to leave, but she was nervous about raising a baby by herself. A few nights before she died, we got a little drunk at the bar, and I kissed her. I was falling in love with her, and it just felt right at the time, I guess. But she backed away and said she couldn't handle another relationship right now and ran out. I sat there, my heart in my hand, crushed. Then angry, I guess.

"I called her a few days later, the day she died, in fact, to have her meet me back at Vinny's so I could tell her how I felt and make her feel that same embarrassment she had made me feel just days before." His apparent empathy for Brandon began shifting to the anger he felt for Ella. "I wanted her heart to hurt as bad as mine did, I'll admit it. But she never showed. Next day, the town was buzzing with the news of her disappearance. I got called down to the police station a few times for questioning, and I told them exactly what I just told you. I don't know exactly what happened that night, but she wouldn't have just up and left town like that, given that she stood to get all that family's money. No way. That's why I knew then she was dead."

Chad looked him straight in the eye as he said those last words, as if trying to drive a final nail in the coffin. He almost looked happy knowing she would never come around again. But Brandon had a suspicion that he was hiding something. He had a slight smile on his face while he told his version of the story. He looked angered, but yet satisfied in a way, Brandon noted.

Brandon suddenly felt uneasy about being in Chad's

house with Maddie. He squeezed her hand under the table, letting her know to follow his lead.

"Well, thanks for talking with us. I'm just trying to get closure for myself, you know? I don't know much about her and thought it would be good to find out whatever I could," he said, hoping that his outward confidence would cover up the sudden fear he felt inside.

Brandon stood up, and Maddie followed his cue, standing next to him while she waited for his next move. He reached over to shake Chad's hand. Chad did not stand up, his eyes and cocky smile locked on Brandon.

"We can let ourselves out. Thanks for your time." Brandon quickly turned around and led himself and Maddie out the door. They walked to the Jeep, careful not to say another word out loud.

Chad stood in the doorway watching them. He had hoped he would never hear her name again after that night. A night he would never forget. And one that he wouldn't go into any detail about with anyone, certainly not her own son. Ella made a fool out of him, and he was glad she was dead and gone. He could feel the anger and tension building up inside him like a steamship ready to blow. *It wasn't the kid's fault his mom was a whore, but Ella got what she deserved,* he thought to himself as he continued to eye Brandon.

As Brandon backed out the driveway, he turned his head back to the house one last time to see Chad leaning against the doorjamb watching their moves, giving both of them an eerie feeling.

Brandon sped off from the driveway back toward the farm. "Sorry, Maddie, I shouldn't have taken you there," he said, breaking the silence between them, feeling guilty for putting her in a potentially dangerous situation.

She took his hand and nodded nervously with a smile. She didn't want him to feel bad about dragging her along. She felt an obligation to be there for him in case he needed her. The fear she felt sitting across from Chad had been palpable. She couldn't shake the feeling that something terribly wrong had happened at this man's hand, but she didn't have the courage to tell Brandon yet. She decided it was best to let it simmer for now. Taking a deep breath in and letting it out, she repeated this several times to gain her control back as they drove to the farm.

Brandon could not help but replay the conversation in his mind. If Chad's story were true, he wondered what his mother would have ever seen in him or why she trusted him. And why was she so unhappy with Jimmy? It seemed, to him anyway, that Jimmy was doing what he thought would bring her happiness. Wasn't that enough? Or was there something there he didn't know? He needed a good way to broach the subject of their marriage with Jimmy, a subject that Jimmy had made clear in the past that he did not wish to speak about. Jimmy had moved them to the city so abruptly after his grandmother has passed away, running as fast as he could from the only place that Brandon ever knew and loved. And Brandon tried to live his life as if nothing was missing, when in fact, the biggest part of his life was gone. Maybe he didn't care to feel the pain either. But things were different now. Pandora's box had been opened, and Brandon owed it to his mother and to himself to dig inside and find the truth.

"Something just isn't sitting right with me, Maddie," he said as they pulled into the driveway at the cabin. "I'm gonna ask Jimmy about his marriage to my mom. I need to know why she was so unhappy. I'm sure he knows about Chad, too."

A sudden feeling of anxiety formed in the pit of his stomach. Instincts were telling him that his mom was brutally murdered. Here. In this town. And he had a feeling that no one wanted to find the truth. The truth meant that this small town would forever bear a nasty scar, one that could never be repaired, and the town wasn't ready to wear that kind of mark.

"Maddie, I think he's here, living in this town, walking amongst everyone, having normal conversations. Just living his life as if nothing ever happened," Brandon spoke, looking into the woods in the distance.

"Who?" Maddie asked, looking at Brandon, fearing what he was about to say.

"My mother's murderer."

Chapter Eleven

Brandon sat in his room back at the cabin for what seemed like an eternity to Maddie. She sat on the edge of the couch, clasping her hands in her lap, waiting for him to emerge from his bedroom. She prided herself on knowing what to say and when to say it, but she was at a loss for words. Her best friend, whom she knew better than anyone else, was overwhelmed, and she was powerless to help him. And although he didn't know it, she was completely in love with him, complicating matters even further. She feared she would lose him if he poked around too much in this town.

She bounced her heels up and down on the floor beneath her, desperately trying to think of what to do next. *Love is a tricky emotion*, she thought. *It can open your eyes and yet still have the ability to cloud your mind all at once.*

The doorknob to Brandon's bedroom clicked as he turned it, jolting her out of her thoughts. He emerged stone-faced into the living room and sat beside her, mindlessly looking out the window.

"Brandon?" she asked, placing her hand on his back for comfort, "is there anything I can do to help you? I can put on a pot of coffee for us, or we can make something to eat if you're hungry?" she asked, desperate to offer something that would soothe his soul.

"I'm okay, Maddie," he replied, turning his head to focus on her eyes, "just had to think about what to do next.

Brandon felt silly for his silent reactions thus far, perhaps overreacting and overthinking the whole situation. It was possible that his mother just disappeared, wasn't it? He looked into Maddie's golden eyes and reminded himself that this was her vacation too, not an episode of *Dateline* where they try to uncover a killer. He couldn't drag her into his past; she had enough to deal with in her own personal life.

"Buuuut, I can't think without food, so what did you have in mind?" he asked, squeezing her knee before standing up and heading over to the kitchen area.

"Uh..." She realized she hadn't thought about what to offer when she had asked if he was hungry. "Well, how about we make this a team effort and rummage through the kitchen to see what we can make together? It'll help us both relax, I think."

If Maddie knew anything at all, it was that spending time making food in the kitchen was a great way to decompress and remove yourself from reality for a moment. She had spent years doing this for herself and found it therapeutic. She loved that she and Brandon could share the joy of cooking, even though he admitted he wasn't great at it.

Brandon flipped on the small stereo that sat on the windowsill, a small CD player that still worked, surprisingly. The soft, sultry sounds of Billie Holiday gently filled the space inside the cabin, removing whatever tension was left in the room.

Evan had arranged for groceries ahead of their arrival, so the kitchen was stocked with the basic essentials. Brandon pulled out a box of farfalle and a jar of sauce from the pantry while Maddie found a package of fresh beef in the fridge. There were a few bottles of wine in a rack above the fridge, and the two of them settled on merlot to go with the pasta they decided to make.

Brandon poured them each a generous glass and handed one to Maddie.

"Cheers to my best friend, one of the most beautiful and thoughtful people I have ever met." He tipped his glass slightly to meet hers and winked as they took their first sip. The sweet liquid instantly warmed his body and sent a riptide of tingles through every nerve in his body.

She looked incredible tonight, in her cream-colored sweater and jeans. She wore a gold necklace with her name etched in the middle, where her collarbones met. Brandon suddenly found himself fighting the urge to kiss her. It wasn't the first time he had thought about it; she was, after all, the most sought-after woman on campus. But this felt different, like a primal urge that almost couldn't be contained. *Not now, Brandon, just enjoy the moment.* He turned his attention to the pot of boiling water on the stove and added the pasta.

Maddie kept herself busy setting the table, finding her way through shelves and drawers for the necessary table-ware. She located a package of candles and a beautiful, silver candelabra to place in the middle of the table to create the perfect ambience. Brandon joined her, serving up plates of pasta with sauce, and the two of them sat down for dinner.

They talked about school, his memories of the farm, their time back in Pennsylvania as children. Anything and everything that came to their minds, except for his mom and the nightmares.

Brandon finished his last bite, picked up the wine glass, and swished around the contents inside. He sat back in his chair before taking another sip. He smiled at Maddie in admiration. He loved that the two of them could talk for hours, yet it seemed only minutes would pass by on the clock. He imagined that she would be his perfect mate in life, the kind anyone would dream of. He watched her as she got up and headed to the freezer to get the rum raisin ice cream out, a favorite for them both, bringing back memories from holidays before when the two of them would consume an entire gallon of the sweet dessert by themselves.

Brandon quickly cleared the table and stoked the fire so they could sit in front of it and finish the wine and dessert. He threw down a wool blanket on the floor in front of the hearth and invited her to sit down with him.

As they finished the last of the ice cream and consumed the last of the wine, Brandon found himself with enough courage to lean over and kiss her lips. *I can't believe I'm doing this!* Her lips were soft and her tongue was warm and sweet. He slowly pulled back and leaned against the pillow he had propped up on the side of the couch. He instantly felt a moment of regret for taking advantage of the moment.

This was his best friend. What he really willing to risk their friendship over his desire for her? *What am I doing? She doesn't want this.*

"Maddie, I—" She gently placed a finger on his lips to silence his next word and leaned in to kiss him again. An intense fire burned within him as the kiss became longer. She tasted better than he could have imagined, and he never wanted this moment to end. Brandon stopped for a moment and looked at her, the glow from the fire illuminating one side of her face.

With the courage from the wine on his side, he said to her, "Maddie, I need to say something to you." He caressed her cheek with the back of his hand. "I have had a crush on you since the moment you stepped on the bus in the ninth grade. I didn't want to tell you because I was afraid I'd lose you, but I can't go on without you knowing." *Ugh! Stop now, Brandon, you fucking idiot! She is going to pull away!*

She smiled and kissed him on the lips and replied, "I felt the same way. I don't know when exactly I knew, but I just knew." Maddie was no stranger to dating through high school and college, but no one made her feel the way she did with Brandon. But she knew Brandon had refused to go out with any girl and didn't ever seem interested in love. She always felt a tinge of guilt when she would go on dates from time to time, but now she knew why.

"Listen, I want to do this Maddie, but I can't right now." Guilt overpowered his urge to take her into his arms and make love to her. He didn't want their friendship to get weird and sex had a way of making things complicated.

Maddie rested her head on his chest and he ran his fingers through hair. "I get it, Brandon."

He could sense the disappointment in her voice. Brandon pulled her chin up so that he could look her in the eyes. "I don't want to lose you." He wanted so badly to tell her how much he loved her at this moment. To kiss her all night. To tell her how much she meant to him. But he held back. Instead, he kissed her forehead. He put his legs up on the couch and Maddie snuggled in next to him.

They laid together in silence watching the flames gently lick the logs until they became embers. Their eyes fluttered until they each fell asleep in each other's arms, leaving their worries on the other side of the front door for the moment.

Brandon woke up out of a deep sleep a few hours later, still lying on the floor with Maddie. The fire had died down and the room was dark, except for the glow of the moonlight that pierced through the front windows. He peered down at Maddie, who was resting on his chest, and kissed the top of her head. She stretched and opened her eyes to look up at him.

"What time is it?" she asked lazily, glancing around for a clock of some sort.

"Not sure," he replied, getting up and holding his hand out for her to join him as they walked back toward the bedroom, each of them wrapped in the extra blankets from the couch to shield them from the cold air outside the boundaries of the fireplace. When Maddie turned to go to her room, Brandon tugged at her hand gently. "Stay with me?"

She smiled and followed him into his bedroom. As they

settled down in Brandon's bed together, Brandon turned to her, propped his head up on his hand, and said, "I'm thinking I need to walk over to Grandma's house tomorrow and see if I can get Jimmy to talk to me about my mom." He knew it was a sensitive subject for Jimmy. "It's just, every time I wake up from one of these dreams, I get these awful headaches now. I thought at first it was just a side effect of drinking or something, but I'm feeling them more frequently even when I'm awake. I feel something's wrong," Brandon continued as he mindlessly played with the ends of her hair.

"You know, Bran, if you suspect foul play, we could take a ride down to the police department and see if they have the old case files on your mom. Maybe they know something or you'll see something in the files that they didn't catch. Something maybe only you would know. Even something from those weird dreams."

"Actually, that's not a bad idea. I hadn't thought about that," he said, bringing her in closer to his body and kissing her forehead. "After I talk to him in the morning, we can take a ride down to the barracks." He hesitated a little and then added, "I...I think I need to talk to Jimmy alone, though. He may be more reluctant to give me information if you're with me."

"I understand," she said reassuringly, reaching her head up to kiss him again. She was hopeful they could solve this together so that Brandon could get the closure he so desperately deserved.

They didn't utter another word to each other but instead just held each other. Brandon watched her face in the shadows as she drifted off to sleep once more.

Brandon felt a deep responsibility to keep her safe now, but as he watched her sleep, he felt an uneasy pit forming inside his stomach. Trouble loomed outside of the walls of the cabin. He sensed an evil lurking in the woods, watching their every move, waiting for just the right moment to draw them into the darkness.

Chapter Twelve

Brandon woke at sunrise and quietly got out of bed to get ready. He pulled the covers gently over Maddie, careful not to disturb his sleeping beauty. He wanted to get over to his grandma's house to catch Jimmy before he left for the market. Thanksgiving was just a few days away, and there was a rainstorm approaching in the area later in the evening. After getting dressed, Brandon exited the bedroom and walked to the kitchen. He located a notepad and penned a quick note to Maddie, letting her know of his plans, signing it "Love, B." He placed it next to the coffee machine and then turned to grab his jacket and head out the door.

Brandon stepped out on the sun-drenched porch and stopped for a moment, taking in the beauty of the morning. The air felt warm against his face, slightly humid from the impending storm but otherwise refreshing. He scanned the fields and the small pond just past his grandma's house. The ravens picked through the dead grass for any scraps they could find. He almost found it hard to believe that such horror could ever have existed here, but this small town with its pretty face held ugly truths behind the façade. A killer was still breathing here and likely living a normal life, he reminded himself, and he needed to find him...or her. He breathed in one long breath and continued down the steps and across the lawn to the main house. As he made his way towards the roundabout in front of the house, he heard a rustling in the woods behind him. He stopped in his tracks and turned around to survey the area. He stood quietly for a few moments, realizing that if there were any danger, there was nothing to protect him from where he stood.

His ears pricked as he strained to listen, and suddenly, he heard the snapping of twigs just past the back of the cabin. He frantically looked around for something to defend himself and found a small rock. It was better than nothing, he thought, picking it up from the ground, holding it tight in his right hand as he walked back towards the cabin to the place where he heard the noise. His heart pounded faster, the adrenaline now pumping through his veins. He heard the footsteps again, coming closer toward the house. He walked around the corner of the house to the backyard, keeping the cabin close to his back. Just then, a figure came around the other corner.

"Hello, Brandon!" Evan shouted, his deep voice startling him.

Brandon realized he had been holding his breath and let it out, hoping Evan didn't notice his panic. He reached down, pretending to wipe something off the bottom of his pant leg so he could drop the rock he had picked up for protection. He suddenly felt foolish.

"Hi there, Evan!" he replied, wiping his clammy hands on his coat before offering one of them to Evan.

"Sorry, son, I hope I didn't wake you and your lady friend," Evan said as he began fussing with a piece of siding on the house. "I noticed this wood beginning to rot the other day, and I wanted to get it fixed before I have an even bigger issue on my hands." He grabbed a tool from his tool belt and started about his job.

"No, no, it's fine. I was already awake. I was about to head up to see Jimmy before he heads out to the market."

Evan was already hard at work, carefully removing the old wood. Brandon could tell that he took the work here seriously and didn't miss a beat, even after all these years. Evan had been living at the guest house since before Brandon was born. He had helped his grandmother take care of the property since her husband had passed and knew every inch of the land he cultivated.

As a child, Brandon would pepper him with incessant questions about the work he was doing, always curious. Brandon was particularly interested in the horses back then and used to try and help him in the stables when he had the opportunity.

His grandma had once owned six Irish Draughts, mostly brown and gray, except for a single white mare they called Princess. She had grown up riding the horses, showing them from time to time, and didn't give it up when she had married George. But the horses had all seemed to disappear after Ella died. Brandon overheard his grandmother on the phone one day telling someone that she had decided to sell them. She felt they weren't getting enough attention from her, and she could not devote any more of her time to the art of raising and showing them. Perhaps she was overwhelmed with grief or maybe it was because she already knew the cancer was invading her body. Brandon never knew the exact reason, but he understood them just the same.

"The farm seems so different with all of the animals gone, doesn't it?" Brandon asked, sparking gentle small talk.

Without looking away from what he was doing, Evan responded, "I suppose, but it was time. No one, except myself of course, was taking care of these animals anymore. It is a lot for one person."

"Yeah, I guess so," Brandon continued. "I know my mom would have been sad to know that Princess was sold if she were still here—"

"But she isn't here, is she? She can't be sad if she isn't here," he interrupted Brandon, appearing to lose patience.

Brandon looked at him with wide eyes, taken aback by his abrupt statement. He remembered that Evan wasn't much for talk. He never was, even when Brandon was a child. Evan wasn't a man of compassion. He was built to work, not to comfort.

"Sorry, I know you're busy, so I'll just get to the point," he replied. "And since you mention it, I'd love to know what you can tell me about my mom. It would really help me close the chapter on her."

"Well, I don't know much about her. I didn't engage in long conversations with her, but I do remember her moping about the place after your dad was killed. She'd just walk around here with you in her arms, not really sayin' much. She didn't ask for much either. She found herself going to the bar almost every night, drinking by herself, 'til she found that man and then disappeared or got herself killed. That's when hell broke loose. Maybe she was just trying to get away from here, I dunno. Don't think she was too happy 'bout being here, if I'm being honest. Farm life isn't for everyone, ya know?

"Your grandma dumped this farm on your mom and dad just a year or so before you were born, but when your dad was killed, all that pressure mounted on your mom. I got the feeling she was overwhelmed, not that she had much to do, since I take care of all the grounds here," he said, proudly.

"Anyway, I asked her once if she'd ever consider selling it to me, you know, so I could take the burden off her? She didn't seem all that interested in selling, maybe because your grandma was still alive, or she had shacked up here with Jimmy."

"Do you remember anything from the night she disappeared?" Brandon asked.

"Nope," he replied without hesitation. "I wasn't here that night. I had taken one of the Irish mares up to Syracuse to a man who had purchased her from your grandmother. I decided to stay up there a few days to help him along with his new horse. By the time I got back, this town had already gone crazy with her disappearance. Police everywhere, local news folks jammin' up the entrance to the farm looking for answers, complete chaos. Police questioned me too, but I wasn't much help. That's really all I know, kid," he finished and returned his attention back to the siding on the house.

Brandon couldn't help but feel disappointed, though he wasn't surprised that the answers would not come so easily. Why would they? If people knew what had happened to her, they would have said something by now, wouldn't they?

He thanked Evan for his help around the farm and turned to continue his walk back toward his grandmother's house.

Evan took his eyes off the work he was doing on the house and watched Brandon walk away. He stood up slowly, hesitating for a moment, before calling out to him, "Hey, kid..."

Brandon's heart skipped a beat, hopeful he'd share something that hadn't previously been known. He turned around, placed his hands in his pockets, and casually walked back to Evan, eager to hear what he had to say.

"I've been working this farm for almost forty years now and don't really see an old man like myself settling down anywhere else, ya know? I could take this place off your hands, if you wanted. I'm not tryin' to step on any toes, but a kid like you probably has big city plans. An old farm like this needs a lot of attention. I could give you a fair price, if you were ever interested."

Brandon's shoulders slumped slightly, and he emitted a quiet sigh. Though he was grateful for Evan's loyalty at the farm, he wanted more than he could offer. "Thanks, but I think I'm gonna hold on to this place for now. It's the last piece of my family's existence, and I'm just not ready to let go, ya know? I hope you'll still stay on, though. You've been so instrumental in preserving her beauty, and I can't thank you enough," Brandon said, hoping he wouldn't be offended.

Evan didn't respond but instead nodded with under-standing and turned back to the siding on the cabin. He got back to work hammering the fresh plank of wood on the house.

Brandon turned once more to walk away, carrying with

him the conversation he just had with Evan. Perhaps Evan was right. Brandon had worked so hard on his schooling and had an entire plan already mapped out. This farm was never part of it, and he didn't know the first thing about taking care of a property, let alone a massive farm in the woods. The thought of it suddenly became daunting, and Brandon quickly pushed it to the back of his mind. He had enough on his plate right now and didn't need to dwell on the farm just yet. He stopped at the bottom of the stairs to his grandma's front porch, took a sharp breath, and exhaled, "Let's do this."

He walked up the stairs and opened the front door, stepping into the foyer.

"Dad?" he called out, hoping he didn't startle Jimmy.

Jimmy came walking out of the kitchen, drying off a paring knife he had just washed with a kitchen towel, a plain look on his face, as if Brandon had caught him in the middle of deep thought.

"Morning, Dad," Brandon said, giving him a half hug. "Did I catch you at a bad time?"

"Huh? Uh...oh, yes." Jimmy's faced warmed with a smile as he snapped out of his thoughts and returned to reality. "Sorry, kiddo, I was just trying to run through the menu for Thursday and make breakfast at the same time. I have a lot on my mind, I guess. You want something to eat?" he asked, turning to walk back toward the kitchen.

"That sounds good," Brandon replied, though he wasn't in the mood to eat. *Hard conversations are best served over food*, he thought. He followed him into the kitchen and sat at the small, 50s style kitchen table in the middle of the room.

Jimmy returned to the vegetables on the cutting board and resumed chopping them to make omelets. A favorite of his anytime they vacationed.

"Listen, Dad, I know you don't like when I bring up Mom." He paused for a second, not wanting to waste much time, getting right into his questions. "But I've been thinking about her lately, and I just feel like, I dunno...I guess I just want to know more about her."

Jimmy stopped cutting his mushroom, put the knife down, and stood there with his back still facing Brandon. "Alright then, let's get on with it," he replied with a noticeable edge in his voice. "What do you want to know?"

"What do you think happened? Everyone I've spoken to in this town seems to think she's dead, except for you. Why is that?"

He slowly turned toward Brandon, his lips small and his gaze intense. "Your mom and I weren't gettin' along," he began, his expression turning solemn. "I tried so damn hard to make her happy, but it wasn't enough. Instead of being a happily married couple, we became a pair of roommates, taking care of a baby and nothing more."

His body leaned back into the counter, and he crossed his arms. "I'd watch you by day with your grandma, and your mom would take care of you at night, so that I could work. She took good care of you when she had you, but sometimes I think the pain of your dad being gone was just too much for her to bear. That night she left, we had a big fight. Never told anyone that except for you, now that I think of it. I was so afraid the police would think I did something if I mentioned it, so I never said a word. She wanted a divorce. Said she was miserable and wanted to start over.

She said"—his words broke off for a moment—"she said she never should have married me in the first place." Tears welled up in his eyes. "All I ever wanted for her was to make her happy and raise you. I promised your dad that if anything happened, I would do that for him."

He wiped his eyes with the back of his hand and turned back to the cutting board, picking up right where he left off.

"I did what I thought was honorable, and she just shit all over me," he continued, his tone becoming sour and his chopping efforts audibly faster and louder. "I gave her everything, and she left me nothing but heartache. When I came back from work that night, I found you sleeping soundly in your bed, and she was gone. Your grandma said your mom had wanted to get out for a drink and that she shouldn't be long, but I knew something wasn't right. She was never gone for that long. I found a note on a ripped piece of paper next to the phone," he said, stopping once again to reach into his back pocket for his wallet.

He rummaged through the billfold and pulled out a worn, folded piece of torn paper and walked it over to Brandon. Brandon stood up to take the paper from his hand, carefully opening it to reveal his mom's handwriting. *I'm sorry. Please forgive me.*

He stared at the words, trying to digest each one's meaning. It didn't make sense to Brandon, and he wondered if something was missing or if this was all she had left to say.

"You never questioned this? Never showed it to the police? Come on, Dad!" His voice rose as a pinch of anger began to pull inside him. "This note doesn't say shit, and you just assume she left us?"

Jimmy slammed his hand on the counter, his brow furrowed and his cheeks burning red.

"What else was I supposed to think, Brandon? Huh? Listen to me, kid. She left. She didn't love me, and she was too consumed with grief to handle you. If she were dead, they woulda found her body. I did the best I could to try and shield you from this, I really did, but you've opened that door, and now here you go! Your mom doesn't deserve me, and she sure as hell doesn't deserve the time and effort you're putting into asking all these questions! You know, wh—"

"Don't talk about my mother like this!" Brandon interrupted, moving closer to him, his face mere inches from him. He stared him squarely in the eye, his voice leveling out. "Just because she disappeared doesn't mean she didn't love me and walked out. You know what I think? I think you just let her go and didn't care. That's what I think."

Brandon stepped back toward the table, waiting for a response.

Jimmy's breath still heavy from anger, he replied in a low voice, "I raised you like you were my own. I gave you everything and I didn't have to do shit for you. You would have been an orphan if it weren't for me! You know what I think? I think you're just as ungrateful as she was."

Jimmy pushed Brandon and stormed outside, the front door slamming against the frame.

Brandon sat back in his chair at the table, placing his face in the palms of his hands, and began to sob. He suddenly felt so alone.

Chapter Thirteen

Brandon felt paralyzed in a room that seemed to be spinning around him. Every thought he had about his stepdad came rushing to the front of his mind and put into question like an interrogation. He felt as though he didn't even know him anymore.

And the note? It seemed too suspicious. His memory of his mother was always fresh on his mind, and he knew she would never leave a half-assed note like that. His mother loved him, of that he was sure.

The room stopped spinning and his thoughts began to return to their respective spaces in his mind. He stood up and suddenly felt angered and betrayed. He was foolish for trusting Jimmy all these years. How could he have missed it? He had been so sour over the mention of her name and wanted nothing to do with her whereabouts.

Brandon began to wonder if he helped cover up her death, or worse, if he killed her himself.

He shuddered at the last thought and tried to remind

himself not to overreact. *Time to get Maddie.* He took a deep breath and headed out toward the cabin.

Maddie sat on the porch bundled in the thick wool blanket she found in the chest in the bedroom. She took a sip of her coffee and looked out to the farm in awe as she waited for Brandon to come back. Her mind replayed every second of the night before, and she found it difficult to control her smile at the thought of her and Brandon together. His cologne still lingered on her skin and teased her senses in between sips of coffee.

Suddenly she heard a door slam from across the lawn. She watched as Brandon emerged from the front door at his grandma's house, and she stood to wave to him, her smile fading as she saw the angered look upon his face. She put her blanket and coffee down on the table next to the rocking chair and walked to the top of the steps.

Brandon walked up the steps, passed Maddie without so much as a hello, and stormed into the house. The storm door slammed against the frame with a loud crack that echoed through the forest. She ran inside after him.

"Brandon, are you okay?" she asked, his back facing her as he stood at the kitchen counter.

"I don't even know where to start, Maddie," he said, his voice sounding confused. "I think he's hiding something from me. I went over there to talk to him and he just blew up! And his face, Maddie..." He turned to her. "It was filled with so much hatred and anger. I thought he could have killed me right then and there, just for saying her name!"

Maddie walked over and placed her hands on Brandon's shoulders, looking up at his eyes. "Okay, Bran," she started, urging him to take a deep breath with her. "He's probably never dealt with his emotions over her before today. Don't think the worst of him yet, okay? He took care of you...and me, for that matter. I don't think a killer would be able to look in the eyes of a child whose mother he murdered," she added.

"Come on, Maddie. You think a murderer feels anything? He could have done it out of spite and enjoyed it for all I know. It happens all the time!" Brandon's heart pumped faster at the thought of someone hurting his own mother.

"Okay, okay, I get it," she said, moving in to embrace him. She stood with him for a few moments in silence before continuing, "Let's just get in the car and head down to the police like we planned. Let's see what they know first before we make any assumptions. This is a small town. I'm sure everyone there will remember and have some insight into what happened that night." She pulled back from the hug, leaving her hands on his arms to give him a gentle squeeze before turning around to get her coat.

Brandon reached for her shoulder as she began to walk away and gently turned her back around, bringing her back to him for another embrace. "I'm sorry, Maddie," he said, realizing that he must have come across as a madman, "it's... it's just that I freaked out a little. I've never seen that side of him before. I didn't mean to alarm you or brush you off, if I did." He kissed the top of her head, holding her tighter as he took in her scent. "We'd better get going."

They put their coats on in silence, preparing for their journey to the barracks. Brandon opened the door, motioning for her to head out first. The air was still and quiet, dark clouds beginning to fill the sky, as an impending rainstorm approached from the distance. Brandon looked around to see if Evan was still tinkering with the house, but he had already left. They got in the Jeep and headed out to the police barracks.

The barracks were located just off the main road, about ten minutes from the farm. Brandon and Maddie spent the time riding in the car talking aimlessly about the town, avoiding the subject of his mom's case.

Maddie was falling in love with the town and the farm, despite the dark history. Spending time outside of the city as a young girl was not something that she ever had the opportunity to do given her circumstances. The cabin felt warm to her, and the area was serene, like a piece of Heaven here on Earth. Everything about this town felt special including her love for Brandon. It felt real. She wanted to kiss him again this morning but hesitated when she saw how upset he had been from his visit with Jimmy.

Brandon admired her excitement for his hometown. She had an untainted view of the place from her own lens. He hoped that by digging up the past, it would not tarnish her view forever, or his own. The idea that events so horrific and tragic could have happened to his own loved ones here was almost unfathomable, but he knew that even small towns were capable of carrying dark secrets.

Maddie pointed her finger to a single-story, brick building coming up on their left, in the middle of a cleared field. "That looks like the station. I see the sign up ahead."

The small building looked fairly new. The parking lot entrance had a digital sign that read *Welcome to Troop F Police Station*. The parking lot was painted with fresh parking paint. The roof was made with modern black aluminum panels.

Brandon parked in front of the building, and they headed in the automatic sliding door, where they were greeted by a friendly, older lady who introduced herself as Helen.

Helen was dressed in a light pink cardigan and black slacks. Her bleach blond hair was neatly tucked in a bun. She wore blue eyeshadow and mascara as thick as tarantula legs. Her heavy perfume permeated the lobby.

Brandon introduced himself and Maddie and casually asked to see someone he could talk to about a disappearance twenty years earlier.

The plastered smile melted into a frown as she contemplated what to say next.

"My goodness..." she replied, mindlessly grabbing her shirt over her heart and letting out a quick sigh. "There has only been one disappearance in this town, one we will never forget," she continued, shifting her eyes to the distance, as if reliving the events of that day. "Sweet girl. Such a shame it went cold. Her name was Ella."

Chills rippled through Brandon's body like waves in the ocean at the mere mention of his mother's name from this stranger's lips. "Yes, that's her," he said.

"Forgive me for being so blunt, but you seem a bit young to be a reporter, sniffing around an old case like that one. A small town like this doesn't need to relive the pain by ripping open an old wound. We've tried to move on from it, if you know what I mean."

He didn't. He could never understand why anyone in

this town would just want to ignore something so tragic, blowing it off as if nothing ever happened.

"I'm Brandon Stone. Ella Arroyo Stone-Callahan was my mother," he said, enunciating every syllable in her name.

Her inquisitive face returned to the overly joyful look with the plastered smile as she connected the dots in her mind. "Holy smokes! I didn't see the resemblance right away, but now I see those distinct Stone family features! Such a great-looking family. I'm so sorry about your mama," she said, putting her hand out on the counter in front of her, as she offered her condolences. She picked up the phone, pushed a few buttons, and waited for someone to pick up at the other end of the line.

"Andy...we have someone here to see you." She stared at Brandon, as she "mmm-hmmm'd" her acknowledgement to Andy's questions a couple of times. A few seconds later, she hung up the phone and invited them to sit down on the bench directly across from her desk and wait for the chief to come and see them.

After several uncomfortable silent minutes, a portly man emerged at the end of the hallway. His sideburns and base of his head were peppered in black and gray which contrasted his dark, copper-colored skin. He had a serious yet somehow warm look on his face as he approached the bench where they sat. Maddie stood up as he got closer, gently nudging Brandon to do the same.

Chief Andrew Walker introduced himself in a deep, husky voice, offering his large, chubby hands to them both, his grip firm but not overbearing. He opened a door just next to the bench and led them into a large conference room. There was an oblong table in the middle, with empty office chairs neatly lined around it. Brandon and Maddie took a seat at the chairs nearest the door, while Chief Walker walked to the opposite end and sat at the head of the table facing them.

"What can I do for you today?" he questioned.

"I'm here to ask you some questions about my mother's disappearance twenty years ago. I'm hoping you remember the case and can tell me anything you know about what happened," he replied, getting right to the point.

The chief sat back in the chair, resting his hands on his round belly, contemplating what to say next. "Your parents were fine people," he began, "they were well known in this town and loved by everyone. It was a shame what happened to them both in a relatively short amount of time."

"Thank you, Chief," Brandon acknowledged nervously. He suddenly felt hot and pulled at the sweater he wore, which now felt as though it were strangling his neck.

Maddie reached into her purse and pulled out a small bottle of water, offering it to him without saying a word. She waited for him to open it and take a sip; meanwhile, they listened to the chief's words.

"I was the lead detective on the case for your mother. Remember it like it was just yesterday, in fact. That moment nearly changed my life, you know? Almost wrecked me personally and professionally. Not sure what I can tell you, but I'll do my best."

"We combed every inch of this town, sent out the dogs, enlisted every volunteer we could, and found nothing. It was as if she opened the door to the house, stepped out, and just vanished into the night," he said, looking out the window to the bare trees behind the barracks.

"What about interviews?" Brandon asked. "Did anyone talk to Jimmy? Or that guy, Chad, that she was hanging out with prior to that night?"

"I can assure you that we spoke to everyone that saw her that day. There wasn't any evidence that could tie it back to Jimmy, or anyone else for that matter. Besides, Jimmy isn't the killing type anyway. And Chad?" A half smirk on his face, he shook his head in disbelief. "He was jealous of your mom, sure, but he's harmless for the most part, and his alibi was rock solid. It was most likely a passerby with no previous connection to your mom. Just a cold-hearted criminal with an appetite for killing or kidnapping," he said, though his tone was clear that he was certain she'd been murdered. *People don't just go disappearing like that*, he seemed to silently convey.

Maddie nudged Brandon under the table and leaned in to whisper in his ear, "Tell him about the dream, Brandon."

Brandon suddenly felt embarrassed. He had never told anyone about his dream except for Maddie, let alone a complete stranger, but he had nothing to lose at this point.

He turned back to the chief and told him about his bizarre dreams. He told him about the shed and the woman he saw trapped inside. "I know this sounds crazy, Chief Walker. Trust me, it sounds just as strange to me hearing it come out of my own mouth, but I'm almost certain that the trapped woman is my mom. I think she was murdered here...in this town...and is buried in a shed somewhere close."

The chief had a neutral expression on his face, and Brandon suddenly felt foolish for telling him about his ridiculous dream.

The chief stood up and pushed his chair in with a look indicating that they should do the same.

"I can't imagine losing your parents at such a young age. You never got a chance to know them, and I'm sure that was very hard for you," he said, looking Brandon deep into his eyes. "These dreams you're having could just be anxiety of the unknown, but I'm afraid I can't use that detail to pop this case back open. What I need is hard evidence, not a dream." The chief opened the door and held it open for them to leave.

Brandon stood up with a solemn look on his face. Madeline followed his cue and grabbed their belongings. Brandon hung his head low as he exited the front door, trailing behind Maddie. *Maybe it is just a dream. A terrible and painful dream.*

Andrew stood behind the front window and watched the two of them leave the parking lot. He had never stopped thinking of that case, though the noise of the town subsided shortly after that night. No one wanted a light shone on the case, for fear they would be the next target. And while the death of Zachary Stone just a couple of years prior to Ella was a hunting accident, Andrew felt deep down there must be a connection somehow, but evidence—or the lack thereof—made it difficult for him to make a case of it. Besides, the town board members made it clear they didn't want him to snoop around Zach's case and cause any additional press attention. A town like this one thrived on summer tourism, and the negative image that two murders would bring would surely hurt the town's deep pockets. The guilt Andrew felt was almost too heavy to bear, but the board voted him in as chief and compensated him generously in return for his silence on the matter. The town counted on him to keep them safe. Even if that meant shielding it from the truth.

Chapter Fourteen

Brandon and Maddie drove back to the farm for what seemed like an eternity in silence. Maddie sensed Brandon's discouragement. And for the first time since they became friends, there was nothing she felt she could say or do that would fix the situation. Helpless, she reached over with her hand and placed it on his leg, hoping he would know she was there for him. He looked over and gave her a blank smile acknowledging her but said nothing.

As he turned down Overland Drive toward the Stone Farm, Brandon winced in pain, throwing one hand up to his temple, holding the steering wheel carefully with the other. The headache was back seemingly out of nowhere.

He quickly jerked the steering wheel to pull to the side of the road, threw the gear in park, and bolted out of the vehicle. He leaned up against the side of the Jeep, bent over, with his hands placed upon his knees, breathing in through his nose and out through his mouth in a calculated and slow manner, desperately trying to hold down the bile rising up through his esophagus.

Maddie exited her side of the car and ran around to Brandon, gently rubbing his back.

He stood up, placing a hand on the Jeep for balance. "This has happened to me once before, Maddie, this stabbing pain in my head," he explained, still breathing slowly, his gaze out toward the woods where he spotted a clearing. "Look!"

Brandon pointed in the direction of the woods, ignoring the excruciating pain for a moment in favor of something else. Maddie followed his finger to see a well-worn path amidst the trees across the road from where they had parked.

He reached back into the Jeep and cut the engine, grabbing his keys before closing the door. "I want to see where this path leads."

"Wait." Maddie hesitated and pulled him back toward her. "I don't think we should go in there, Bran," she said, feeling a tingling in her gut.

Brandon saw the crinkle of worry on her brow. "Look, it's going to be okay," he reassured her, rubbing her shoulder. "I just want to see if there's anything of significance here. We won't be long, I promise."

She sighed and looked toward the path. "Okay, but just a few minutes." Brandon nodded in agreement and led them to the path.

The path was no wider than two feet, and the leaves that lined it were tamped down with years of use. They walked side by side through the winding path, each surveying the land around them. The sky above the dome of leafless tree limbs was beginning to fade, and the forest was growing darker with each passing minute. The air was quiet, not even the rustle of an animal scurrying about, or leaves dancing in the breeze. *The quiet before the storm*, Brandon thought to himself, as he slowly led them down the path. He remembered the incoming rain event that the weather person had been speaking about on the news earlier in the week.

They came upon an old, rotted fence, where the path just seemed to end. An old farm fence, broken in some places from years of neglect. "No trespassing" signs were nailed on trees about every ten feet around the perimeter of the fence. Brandon looked at the nearest sign, but no name was listed on the appropriate line. They stopped at the fence and looked beyond to see a clearing just past the tree line.

Brandon suddenly felt a heavy pit form in his stomach, like a weight that sat there, keeping him from moving for a few moments.

He knew this field.

Without having to walk any farther, he knew what lay beyond the trees just off the field. The very field that he had seen in his dreams every night for as long as he could remember. A wave of dizziness washed over him, and he began to feel the nausea setting in again.

Maddie noticed the change in his appearance, "Brandon, I think we should go back," she said sternly, "like, now."

Just then, a rustling of the leaves in the distance caused them both to freeze. Brandon put his right pointer finger to his lips, signaling with his head in the direction of the noise.

He pulled Maddie in closer to him, moving her around towards his back to shield her from whatever lay before them.

His eyes scanned the area, looking for even the slightest of movements. The forest was daunting. The trees bare, stripped of leaves, the branches gnarled in every direction like the bony fingers of a witch's hand. Every tree trunk looked like a body, just standing there, waiting to make a move. His ears strained to hear, but the air was quiet once again. He knew they were being hunted, and he felt vulnerable like a deer, stranded in the middle of a hunter's trap.

"It's probably just a squirrel or some other animal, but let's get out of here anyway," he lied, hoping it was not obvious that he felt just as scared as she was. They quickly started walking back to the Jeep on the same path that led them to the fence.

After several minutes of brisk walking, Brandon could finally make out the Jeep in the distance and felt a sense of relief. They picked up the pace to a small jog to cross the finish line, and Brandon opened the door for Maddie before running around to the driver's side, closing the door, and locking it, sealing off whatever evil existed outside the doors of the vehicle. A quick glance at the dashboard clock indicated they'd only been gone for about thirty minutes, though it had felt much longer. The engine was cold, but Brandon didn't want to waste more time waiting there at the side of the road. He peeled off toward the safety of the cabin, desperate to get Maddie away from there as quickly as possible.

As Brandon pulled into the Stone Farm entrance just a

few minutes later, he turned to Maddie and said, "I need to find a map of this place."

The field they had located was just a half mile down the road, but without the "no trespass" signs being properly labeled, he had no way of knowing who may possibly own that space of land. Brandon thought if he could find the owner, he could get permission to walk the land and see if the shed truly did exist, like the one in his dream.

"I want to go back out there, Maddie," he continued, focused on the road to the cabin, "but you don't have to come out with me if you don't want to." Brandon felt guilty for taking her out there in the first place, after she warned him that she didn't think it was a good idea.

"It's okay, Bran. I'm probably overreacting anyway," she replied, feeling silly for even opening up her mouth about it in the first place. "It's just that it was getting dark, and I've never been in the woods before. I just felt a little unprepared, is all," she said, looking out her window into the darkness, her mind lost in thought. She wondered what being "prepared" might look like for them. Does she conceal a weapon under her coat in case they ran into trouble? Would they even react and defend themselves with a weapon if it all came down to it? She had spent her entire life growing up in the city, and that life did not prepare her for this situation. She never had to worry about bears, wolves, or even hunters. She suddenly felt angry at herself for not taking advantage of the fact that her mom could care less whether she was home or not. She could have snuck off and experienced the wilderness, learned how to protect herself. The feeling of regret was almost too overwhelming, and tears began forming in the wells of her eyes. She quickly wiped them away and dismissed her thoughts. She couldn't take it all on herself anyway.

Brandon pulled into the driveway outside the cabin. He peered over at his grandma's house to see if Jimmy was there, but the house was dark and the truck wasn't parked in front. He felt guilty about their fight earlier that morning. He thought back to his conversation earlier that day with Chief Walker. Maybe he was right. Jimmy may have been upset at Brandon's mom, but he didn't seem like the type to hurt anyone. Brandon convinced himself to move on for the time being. He needed Jimmy on his side right now anyway, to learn as much as he could about life here at the farm all those years ago.

They walked inside the cabin and flipped the switch to illuminate the living room and kitchen. All was just as they had left it earlier that morning, and Brandon released a quiet sigh of relief. *Safe and sound.* They hung the coats and kicked off their shoes by the door. It felt as if the day had run on forever, and all he wanted to do was decompress and let go for a moment.

Maddie was already walking toward the kitchen, when Brandon simply asked, "Wine?" She half turned back to him while still walking, with a smile on her face. She knew.

Maddie located some fresh glasses and began pouring two generous portions of red wine, while Brandon took out some meats and cheeses to snack on. They took their snacks and set up on the table next to the fireplace. Maddie took a seat on the sofa, throwing the blanket on herself, and watched Brandon as he put wood and kindling on the hearth. He took a long match from the matchbox and swiped it against the side of the box. A quick *pffffff click* filled the silent air between them before the flame ignited. He lit the fire with ease and then walked over to the couch to take a seat next to Maddie. They both sat in somewhat of a trance, watching the flames grow and letting the initial effects of the alcohol slowly uncoil the tension.

Brandon turned to Maddie, resting his head on his hand on the back of the couch. "I'm not even sure where to go from here, Mads."

She reached her hand out and traced the lines in his forehead. "We'll figure it out, Brandon," she said reassuringly. "Didn't Jimmy give you a bunch of paperwork the day we got here? Maybe we'll find something in there about the area nearby that can help us." She took another sip of her wine and contemplated for a moment what would happen if they failed. She hoped it wouldn't change Brandon.

Brandon had almost forgotten about the caramel-colored envelope that Jimmy had given him earlier in the week. With everything going on, he hadn't even thought to examine the rest of the contents inside of it. He placed his glass of wine on the table and quickly walked across the house to retrieve it out of the dresser that he had put it in the other day. A few moments later, he returned to the couch, plopping down so fast, Maddie had to raise her glass in the air to keep the contents from spilling out and over the couch. He began removing the papers inside, spreading them out carefully on the table in front of them, like pieces to a complex puzzle waiting to be put together.

There it was in front of him. All of it. Everything he now owned along with the property map. Brandon felt overwhelmed with grief, as if just learning of their demise. He supposed some part of him had believed that his course would change and his mother would have miraculously come back, foolish as that was. Some days that was all he had going for him. Hope was all he ever had, and in this moment, it all seemed to vanish.

Maddie had already begun to sort through the papers while Brandon sat and watched in a daze. She pulled the property map out and opened it up so that each of them had a half splayed out on their laps. "Look, Brandon," she said, her finger moving up and down the bolded dark lines around the area that said *"George and Alice Stone."* "These are the boundaries around the farm, but I can't tell where we were today in relation to the main property."

They moved in closer, examining it carefully. The map had clearly lived through several generations; the paper was thin and delicate, the names of properties were neatly drawn in cursive, each space marked with the owner's first initial and last name. He spotted a large area in the middle of the map labeled *"G and A Stone."* All of the farm and the five hundred acres surrounding it belonged to his grandparents.

Brandon's heart suddenly felt as if it dropped to his stomach like an elevator car that had lost its cables. Assuming the map's accuracy and that his dream was valid, the area they had hiked to belonged to his family. And his mother's body may have been just yards from where they stood earlier that day.

Chapter Fifteen

Brandon lay in bed later that evening, watching Maddie sleep peacefully, her eyelids fluttering around in her deepest sleep like the wings of a butterfly. His mind was consumed with worry. He ran the events of their hike through his head. He wondered how he could search the area without being detected and how he could do it without putting Maddie in danger. Though the property belonged to the family, he wanted to fly under the radar for fear that he was being watched. He needed time to explore, alone. He rolled onto his back, his hands behind his head, and stared off to the ceiling, calculating different plans. His eyes began to feel heavy, and a few moments later he drifted off to sleep and into a dream.

Brandon found himself at the front of the shed this time. The rain was still heavy and drowned out any other sound of the forest. He looked around but could not see anything other than sheets of rain and the bare trees. He took a few steps toward the door, where he noticed a padlock. *Damn!*

Brandon desperately reached up above the door and felt around the edges of the molding with his hand in hopes of finding the key he had found the other night, but to no avail. Desperate, he stepped back and looked along the ground at the base of the shed. He saw a large, smooth, gray rock that didn't seem to belong here, as there were no other rocks around it, only leaves and dirt. He bent down slowly and lifted the rock up from the ground, revealing an indentation from where the rock had sat for many years. In the center of the small depression was an old, rusted key. His heart fluttered with nervousness as he picked it up from the ground.

He quickly glanced around behind him and saw nothing before standing up and going back to the padlock at the door. He inserted the key into the lock, hearing the faint *click* under the noise of the rain. He pulled the lock free from the door and placed it in the pocket of his raincoat. With a deep breath, he reached forward to push the door open and take a step inside out of the rain, and there he saw the woman across from him staring out the back window of the shed.

Brandon's heart beat so loudly, he became unaware of the heavy rain hitting the aluminum roof of the shed, making the sound of a thousand snare drums. He froze in his spot for fear any movement would send her away. He didn't want this dream to end.

She slowly turned toward him, her tear-stained face staring straight into his eyes. Tears streamed down his face though he made no noise. He couldn't believe she was here, his mother, just feet from him! He had so many questions to ask her, but his mouth felt paralyzed and he couldn't make a sound. Instead, he walked toward her. He wanted to touch her skin one more time.

She turned slightly away from him, moving her arm up toward the window, her long finger pointing outside. With her finger still raised, she turned her head to him, her eyes wide with fear.

He peered out of the window where her finger led and saw a body, face down in the leaves behind the shed. NO!

He raced back out the front door to run around to the back of the shed, his heart sinking to the pit of his stomach as he reached the body. The long red hair was stained with mud. He crashed down on his knees next to the body and carefully rolled her over to reveal his beloved Maddie, her face bruised and bloodied.

"Maddie!" he screamed, as he pulled her tightly toward his chest. "HELP!" he screamed desperately, into the sheets of rain and trees, knowing no one would ever hear him this deep into the woods.

Suddenly, her eyes flung open like a rag doll and she screamed, "Behind you!"

Brandon quickly turned his head to see a baseball bat coming crashing down toward his head.

Chapter Sixteen

Brandon flung himself up on the bed, sweating profusely and breathing heavily as if he had just completed a marathon. *Maddie!* He quickly looked over to the other side of the bed to find her sleeping safely next to him. He inhaled a long breath, holding it for a few seconds with his eyes closed, and exhaled, opening them again to full reality. She was safe, and that was all he cared about for the moment. His eyes carefully looked over every inch of her face as she slept.

Suddenly, he felt the warm touch of her fingers on his back. With her eyes still closed, she slowly traced the length of his spine through his shirt like an artist detailing a canvas.

"Sorry, I didn't mean to wake you up," he whispered. He battled his internal thoughts for a moment. "I need to tell you something."

"What is it? Is everything okay?

He hesitated for a few moments. He couldn't tell her about the nightmare, but she had to know how he felt. What

107

if something happened to her? He could not bear the thought. "Madeline, I love you."

Her eyelids slowly opened and a smile emerged on her lips. "I love you, too, Brandon," she replied in a soft voice. "I've always loved you."

She gently grabbed the fabric of his shirt and pulled him down toward her to kiss him. Brandon returned her kiss. Her mouth tasted just as sweet as the first time.

He let his hand slowly run down her body to the top of her thigh. He paused himself from moving further, rubbing his fingers over her skin where his hand had stopped. She pulled back from their kiss and looked at him. Her eyes seemed to glow in the dark like embers. "Keep going," she urged him.

He looked at her with wanting eyes. Brandon didn't know how much more he could hold back. He wanted Maddie in a way he had never wanted another woman before. His body reacted in ways he had not felt before and he wanted to savor every second and every new sensation.

Maddie pulled off her t-shirt and panties, tossing them to the floor with reckless abandon. Brandon followed her lead and removed his clothing, throwing them next to hers in a heaping pile on the floor. He returned to kiss her lips and then began planting kisses down her neck and along her body.

She pushed him slowly over to his back as she moved to cover him. He could feel her heat radiating off of her. Brandon did not want this to end. He wanted this feeling and this moment to carry on forever. *Is this really happening?* He pondered the reality of the moment as Maddie took her time to explore his body just as he had done to her moments before.

"Maddie," he managed to utter her name between labored breaths. He could feel himself coming close to the edge.

In one smooth movement, the two of them joined together. She rocked her hips up and down and he pushed himself up to meet her every move in unison.

Brandon's mind slipped between this moment and the moment he met her. Never in a million years did he think this would happen. It felt like a dream. No. It was even better than a dream, of that he was sure.

He held back as long as his body would allow. The electricity between them sent shock waves through his entire body. He shuddered and released himself just as he felt her let go into her own peaceful oblivion. Maddie crashed beside him for a few moments. Their breath heavy and their skin was slick with sweat.

There was no turning back now, Brandon thought to himself. He would do whatever it took to care for her.

"I love you," she whispered.

Brandon leaned down to kiss her forehead. "I love you, too." He laid beside her with her head nestled between his arm and his chest and listened to her breath as it slowed and she fell back to sleep.

He stared out of the window into the darkness of the night, with only the sound of their breath filling the space in the room before falling back to sleep.

A few hours later, he woke again. Without making a sound, he slowly inched his way off the bed, careful not to wake her from her sleep. Like making his way through a labyrinth, he weaved his way to the kitchen, tiptoeing gently to avoid the creaky wood floor planks of the old cabin so he did not make a sound. The living room was dark, the embers from the fireplace barely visible but still glowing. There was a small kitchen lamp on the counter that they had left on, helping guide him toward the sink where he grabbed a glass out of the cupboard and filled it with cold water from the old farm sink. He looked out of the window above the sink into the darkness behind the house. The moon was full and cast its light just so he could make out some of the bare trees from the forest line. He walked back to the front of the house and peered out the front windows toward his grandma's house. All was quiet with no sign of life, though he knew Jimmy was still there.

Brandon sipped his water as he stared out into the darkness. *I should have known.* He repeated this in his head over and over for a few seconds as he reevaluated his decision to bring Maddie here, knowing he could be putting her in danger. He ran through what he remembered from his most recent dreams, building up to the one from this evening. *What have I done?* He came here to find his mother, but he would never forgive himself if he let anything happen to Maddie in the process.

Brandon finished his drink and headed back to the bedroom and laid back down next to her. He needed to find his mother quickly and get the hell out of here before it was too late for them both.

Chapter Seventeen

Brandon woke once more a few hours later to the sound of the phone ringing that he had left at the side of the bed. Stuck in the area between consciousness and sleep, he pawed around for the phone with his eyes still closed. When his hand finally managed to find the small electronic, he pulled it to his ear and uttered, "Hello?"

"Hey, buddy, I'm sorry to wake you. I..." Jimmy hesitated for a couple of seconds before continuing. He had spent the better part of the previous day feeling like an asshole for blowing up at his only son. It wasn't his fault things ended up this way. "I just wanted to say I'm sorry about what I said yesterday."

Brandon let out a low sigh over the phone before replying, "It's okay, I guess." He still felt sore about their argument and wasn't sure if they could repair what had been broken.

"Listen, I didn't come to fight with you, and I should

have known that this day would come," he responded, hearing the frustration in Brandon's voice. "You have kept very quiet about your feelings, and I shouldn't have pounced on you the way I did. I'm just angry, Bran...*still* angry after all these years. There isn't a day that goes by that I don't think about her and wonder why she's gone. I get enraged when I think of her sometimes, I recognize that, but I can work on it," he continued, his voice hoarse from crying all night. He couldn't lose Brandon as well. He was special, and Brandon had never let him down.

Jimmy quickly changed the subject and began reviewing the menu for their Thanksgiving feast in two days. He had been out in town getting supplies over the last couple of days, wanting to make the remaining time they spent here special. Jimmy tried to imagine what Brandon must be feeling at this moment. Coming back here must not be easy for him, and Jimmy felt he bore some of that responsibility. He never gave Brandon a chance to grieve, just like he never gave himself time to heal. He couldn't wait to get out of here when Ella was gone. But pain doesn't just disappear like hot water evaporating into air. It can only be suppressed in the back of the mind, caged like a wild animal, just waiting for the moment to be let out and take over the senses.

Jimmy continued laying out the plans for the next couple of days and asked Brandon to stop by later with Maddie so they could have dinner together. "Love you, son. I hope you know that," he finished, before hanging up.

Brandon lay quietly in bed next to Maddie for a few more minutes, letting the conversation he just had with Jimmy settle in for a moment. Brandon felt torn between two worlds, the one he thought he knew and the present one. And the only constant was Maddie, the only person he felt he could trust and confide in.

He studied her delicate features as she continued to sleep. Her beauty never ceased to amaze him, and she was even more breathtaking now than ever. He leaned in toward her, gently pushing a lock of hair off of her cheek and then placing a kiss on her lips.

She slowly opened her eyes to see him staring at her with a smile on his face. "Did I sleep too late? What time is it?" she asked, rubbing the sleep away from her eyes.

"It's still early. Jimmy just called here to apologize and then give me the plans for Thanksgiving. He invited us by tonight as well," he said, rolling over onto his back, his eyes focused on the ceiling. "I dunno, I just feel like I can't trust him right now, Maddie. I feel like he's lied to me all this time, really let me down, and I don't know what to do about it."

"You've got a lot on your mind, Bran," she said, moving over to rest her head in the crook of his shoulder. She rubbed her hand over his bare chest. "But you shouldn't jump to conclusions...not yet anyway. We still have some work to do to put this all together."

He turned his head to look her in the eye, "I don't think I should have brought you here. I have a sense that things are going to get heated, and I'm pulling you right into the fire with me," he said, replaying the latest nightmare in his head. He still wasn't sure what his dreams meant, if anything at all. "I love you, Maddie," he stated with conviction in his voice.

She smiled at him. "I love you too," she whispered as she pulled him in to kiss her.

Brandon took in every second of the moment, silently praying to God that it wouldn't be the last he spent with her.

Chapter Eighteen

The two of them got up, showered, and prepared their newest plan over coffee. They both stood with their mugs in hand, resting along opposite sides of the kitchen. Brandon had decided he wanted to visit the cemetery where his father and grandmother were buried. Perhaps something there would strike him...a memory, a premonition, anything to get him closer to his mother's whereabouts. Or maybe he was going crazy. He wasn't sure.

He sipped his coffee, placed the mug on the counter, and turned back to Maddie. "Are you sure you want to do this with me?" he asked, reaching out for her free hand. "You can stay here, lock the doors, and wait until I get back. I can have Jimmy keep an eye on the cabin."

"What are you so worried about, Brandon? I'll be fine. I want to be with you," she replied.

He reluctantly agreed and then made his way toward the front door, Maddie not far behind. They got in the Jeep and headed toward the cemetery.

Pleasant Hill Cemetery was just ten minutes from the farm, tucked back off the main road, surrounded by tall trees. It was a small cemetery with a one-way, horseshoe-shaped driveway. At the ends of the driveway were iron gates, one marked for entry and one marked for exit. Brandon pulled into the entrance gate and drove around halfway toward the back of the cemetery before cutting the engine and getting out to locate the headstones. They quietly passed each tombstone, tiptoeing their way carefully through the centuries-old bones buried deep in the earth below them. In the back corner of the property, separated by a small decorative iron fence no taller than a foot, were a half dozen headstones all grouped around a massive angel statue that was etched in large, uppercase letters: STONE. Brandon could feel his pulse quicken as he approached the family plot, feeling like a little boy again, so small in the world. He recalled the last time he stood before these structures at his grandmother's funeral. He remembered everything and yet remembered nothing of that dreadful day as a young boy. He recalled watching the pall bearers carefully crank the knobs to lower her casket into the damp earth, silent tears rolling down his face, his stepfather's hand giving him a gentle squeeze from time to time. All of the other details of that day had vanished shortly after they played out.

They stopped just in front of the small fence, not crossing the threshold. The two of them stood, hand in hand, in silence for what seemed like an entire rotation of the earth on its axis. Brandon had never been this physically close to his father, and yet somehow the grief he felt for someone he never had a chance to know was almost suffocating. The only image he had of him was the one picture he had of both his dad and his mom, safely tucked away in his red tin box, next to his bed. He wondered if his spirit was with him and could see him at that moment. He closed his eyes and silently pleaded with their spirits. *Dad, please, if you can hear me, I need your help. Please lead me to Mom. I have to find her. She needs me.*

Maddie reached over to squeeze his hand lightly. Without looking at her and with his eyes still closed, he brought her hand up to his lips and held it there for a few seconds before lowering it slowly beside him. He let go and opened his eyes to the plots in front of him.

Brandon took two steps forward, placing his hands on top of his father's headstone, running his fingers over the smooth, polished granite, before doing the same for his grandmother, who had been buried to the right of him. After a few moments, he silently stepped back next to Maddie, took her hand, and led the way back to the Jeep without another word.

As they pulled out of the cemetery, they saw a lady just outside the gates standing next to her car. It was Violet, the server they had met just a couple of days before. Brandon stopped the Jeep next to the exit and put the gear in park. Maddie rolled down her window and gave a friendly wave to her. Violet nervously gave a single wave back and began walking up toward the passenger side window where Maddie sat.

"I'm sorry, I hope I didn't frighten you out here. I saw the two of you out there and didn't want to disturb your time on hallowed grounds. I also come out here from time to time to pay respects to my own friends and relatives." Her hands were shoved down in the pockets of her knee-length, camel-colored wool coat. Her hat pushed the hair close to her eyes as she spoke to them. "Listen, don't take this the wrong way…" she continued, locking her gaze on Brandon, "but I don't think you should be here. I'm not much for superstition, or maybe I am, I dunno, but I would just hate it if I didn't speak what I felt and then something bad happens to the two of you." Her cheeks flushed with embarrassment at her ridiculous confession.

"I appreciate your concern, Violet," Brandon assured her as he carefully moved the gear back to drive, "but I'm sure everything will be just fine." He had so many other questions to be asked and places to see. She was killing the precious time they had to get this done. He said goodbye before slowly beginning to release the pressure on the brake under his foot.

She quickly threw her hands on the window jamb where Maddie sat, startling both Maddie and Brandon and forcing him to slam hard on the brake. They jolted forward a bit. "What happened to your dad was no accident, Brandon," she firmly insisted. "And your mom? That doesn't seem like a coincidence to me either. All I'm saying is, be careful here." And just like that, she turned around and walked away, leaving no room for any further discussion on the matter.

Chapter Nineteen

Brandon sat for a few minutes idling, his foot still depressed on the brake and the car still in gear. Violet had peeled off and left just seconds before, leaving them both stunned and silent. No one had ever mentioned to Brandon that his father's death may have been intentional, and so therefore he had never questioned anything. As far as he knew, his dad went out one morning to do some hunting and was accidentally shot, though they never knew who the bullet belonged to. It was not uncommon for accidents to happen during a hunting season. But what if Violet was on to something? Gripping the wheel with both of his hands and squeezing, Brandon slowly pulled back out on the main road to head back home, his mind consumed with the what-if's.

Brandon broke the silence in the car. "I don't think I can handle all this." He put his left hand at his temple, rubbing it in a circle as he used the other hand to drive. "It's like I don't even know who I am anymore!"

A few moments of puzzled silence again passed before Maddie asked, "Do you think Jimmy ever questioned his death when your mom died just a couple of years later?" Her question pierced the air like a pin popping a balloon.

The Jimmy that Maddie knew had always seemed so honest and caring, like the favored teacher in elementary school that the kids always go back to for advice. She couldn't fathom him harboring any deep secrets about Brandon's past, but maybe he was capable of shielding him from the truth, knowing that it could hurt him. Maddie was no stranger to drama and tragedy in her own life, with her alcoholic mother and unloving, unsupportive family. It was easier to write off a family that didn't care. Actually dealing with the trauma seemed far more tragic.

Brandon continued driving back to the farm, speculating what may have occurred and what may not have happened to his family over the years. Reaching Overland Drive just a short time later, he turned on his blinker and made the familiar turn that led to the driveway.

"Ah!" he screamed, wincing in pain and throwing a free hand up to his left temple. He swerved slightly, the tires screeching briefly as Brandon jerked the Jeep back to correct its path. The pain in his head returned so sharply this time, he had little time to react.

"Brandon?" Maddie shouted, as he pulled over to the side of the road. "Are you okay? Tell me what's wrong!"

Brandon didn't reply but instead held his head in his hands, desperately rubbing his head in hopes it would somehow ease the pain. Maddie rubbed his back and looked out the window. They had come to a stop in almost the exact spot in which they had pulled over the day before for the same problem, like déjà vu.

Brandon raised his head from his hands and peered out the window. "Look!" He pointed to the path. "The same spot as yesterday!" he said, almost to the point of shouting, the pain still hammering away at his temples.

"I noticed it too!"

He realized he must be coming off as psychotic in a way. "Sorry, I didn't mean to scare you. The pain just hits me out of nowhere," he said, trying to mask the pain he was feeling. "These headaches seem to hit me in the same spot on the road."

"I was thinking the same thing." Maddie couldn't deny that Brandon was probably onto something. "Maybe this is an important hint of some kind. Do you think we should hike it out again and try to see what's beyond the fence?" she asked, knowing it could be risky. There was only one way to find out, though, and she knew they had to face it eventually.

The sky was covered in light gray clouds, and it was getting late, but there was still at least another hour or so of light, Brandon thought. His curiosity began nagging at him, taking over whatever rationale he had left. He opened the door and stepped outside, sliding the front seat forward to pull out the hunting knife that he had quietly shoved under the driver's seat. He had found it hidden in the back of the closet earlier that day, feeling slight relief that if he had it with him, he may feel better about them wandering around in the woods. He hooked it on to the belt he wore around his waist and lowered his shirt and coat over it so he wouldn't freak Maddie out while they walked through these unfamiliar territories.

Without uttering another word, the pair were off on the same path that had led them to the old fence the previous day, making swift, quiet steps on the soft earth beneath them, their eyes trained on the forest surrounding them, looking for any sign of life aside from their own. All was eerily quiet, except for the sound of their breath and the quick steps of their feet. The air felt slightly moist, and the sky overhead was becoming ominous as the storm approached the area. Brandon prayed silently they wouldn't get stuck in the mess while they lurked around the land.

Several minutes later, they reached the fence they had discovered yesterday, and the headache, which had finally subsided once they left the Jeep, returned in full force, knocking Brandon to his knees as if someone had slammed him in the head with a heavy object.

"Brandon!" Maddie screamed. "What's wrong? Are you okay?"

Brandon did not immediately answer as she quickly ran to his aid and fell down to his side. He suddenly felt dizzy and nauseous, his skin on fire as if he were about to vomit at that very moment. His body felt too weak to try and get up, so he sat back and leaned against the tree next to him, his eyes closed and his breathing slow and steady as he tried to ward off the bile trying to force its way out of his gut.

He reached in his coat pocket to pull out his cell phone, while Maddie continued to look at him with concern. He looked at the screen as he started to dial 9-1-1, noticing the indicator in the top left-hand corner that said No Signal. "Dammit!" he shouted.

"What's the matter?" The tension in her voice grew more intense.

"We have to get out of here," he responded, as he looked around.

Maddie quickly fumbled around her own pockets to pull out her phone to find the same problem. She had to help him, and fast. She wasn't strong enough to carry him out of here in his weakened state and she needed to get him aid immediately.

"I can't leave you here, Brandon."

"Listen, it's going to be okay. Just take the path back to the Jeep and call for help." His vision became blurry as he tried to look her in the eye. The pain was becoming so intense that his body felt paralyzed.

He reached around his neck and pulled off the necklace that had belonged to his mother, kissing the crucifix before handing it to Maddie. She took the jewelry and clasped it around her neck, placing the crucifix under her shirt. He then took the knife he had shoved in his pants and handed it to her. Her eyes went wide and searched his for an explanation.

"Please? I don't know what is going on, but I'm begging you to just take this and trust me."

"Okay," she agreed as she took the knife and placed it in her waistband.

Maddie grabbed the sides of his face with her hands and kissed him, looking around once more, before running back on the same path that had brought them here. The guilt she felt for leaving him was almost unbearable, but she tried to reassure herself that she was doing the right thing. She picked up her pace to a sprint, dashing through the forest, focusing only on the thump of her feet with each quick stride she made toward the Jeep.

The cool air helped to keep her pace brisk though her lungs still burned from running so quickly. Suddenly, she caught movement out of the side of her eye and stopped in her tracks. She slowly backed toward a tree and looked in each direction when the bushy tail of a squirrel appeared from under the leaves and then scurried up the tree. *It's just a squirrel. Keep going!*

Maddie got back on the path and began running once again. With the Jeep now in view, she heard a loud noise in the leaves behind her. She slowed her pace to a walk and turned her head slightly to see what it was, tripping on a branch in front of her on the path. Maddie fell, catching herself with her hands before her face hit the ground. The knife went flying out of her waistband on impact and landed next to a tree a few feet from her.

She quickly stood up and brushed the leaves from her knees and hands. Her heart pounded inside her ears and her breath was heavy. Maddie walked toward the knife and reached down to pick it up. She quickly had a terrible feeling someone was behind her. She froze in place for a moment, steadying her breath before turning around. *It's probably just another animal. Don't stop, just keep running.*

As she began to turn, she saw something come flying toward her head, and it smacked her with such force she plummeted to the ground, and everything went black.

≈

Back at the trunk of the oak tree where Maddie had left him, Brandon was now huddled over in pain, taking in the cool, fall air in deep breaths as he tried to push out the pain. He sat back on the ground, resting his back against the tree with his eyes closed to keep whatever light remained out of his eyes.

Suddenly, the pain in his head vanished like dust in the wind, the nauseated feeling also subsiding. His eyes flung open and he sat up, looking around as he began regaining control of his body. His hands started to feel clammy with sweat, and a prickly sensation teased the back of his neck and arms, the hair rising up off his skin. Frantically, he looked at his watch.

Twenty-seven minutes had gone by since Maddie left. Something didn't feel right to Brandon. She should have been back by now, he thought.

He quickly jumped to his feet and yelled, "Maddie!" The air remained still and quiet, no response in return. The only movement was that of his hot breath against the cold air, forming quick disappearing clouds.

The feeling of adrenaline began pumping through his veins, and without thinking, he started to run back toward the Jeep, his heart pounding through his chest, his lungs burning with the cool air he took in through his mouth.

After running for a few minutes, he could finally see the black canvas top of his Jeep through the trees. He pushed through the woods, his pace becoming faster as he got closer. He finally emerged from the woods, stopping himself only when he reached the back of the car.

"Maddie?" he cried, walking around to the side of the Jeep where the passenger door remained open.

Only Maddie was not inside.

His heart sank. The most terrifying nightmare of all was playing out in real time. He spun around and looked into the woods, screaming her name, hoping she would emerge from behind him. There was no one. Nothing but the sound of his heavy breath and the beating of his heart.

Chapter Twenty

Brandon quickly rummaged through the Jeep, noticing the contents of her purse had spilled out onto the floorboard of the back seat. Her cell phone dead center in the middle of the mess. *No!*

He turned back to the woods, and tears welled up and spilled down his cheeks. "HELP!" he screamed desperately, his sobs becoming uncontrolled. "Maddie! Please, where are you?"

The silence in return was deafening. Not a falling leaf. Not even a breeze to rattle the branches on the trees. Nothing.

She was gone.

With his head spinning and his pulse quickening with each moment, he started fumbling around in his pocket for the keys. From a distance, he heard the hum of a truck approaching. Brandon ran around the Jeep to the road and threw his hands up, waving them in the air, in hopes that the driver would stop for him. As the black F150 came into view, Brandon realized it was Evan, and he felt a small sense of relief for a familiar face.

Evan crossed the lane and parked in front of the Jeep, quickly cutting the engine and jumping out to help.

"Are you okay, son? Are you broken down?" He asked, as he put on a pair of work gloves that he had pulled out of his coat pocket, ready to help.

"My...My..." Brandon struggled to get the words out of his mouth. "Maddie! She...she's gone!" Tears still flowing from his eyes, his voice was hoarse.

"What? Did you call the police?" he questioned right away.

Brandon shook his head slowly back and forth from left to right, partly to answer Evan's question but also in disbelief. This couldn't be real, he thought. *How can this be happening?*

"Okay, first things first. Let's get your Jeep back to the farm and then we can hop in the truck and look for her together."

"No! I have to stay here! What if she comes back?"

"Son, take a deep breath now! You're not gonna do her any good all wound up like you are. We can retrace your steps and look out there together. You two are in unfamiliar territory. It's possible she just got lost, you know?"

Brandon felt a small sense of relief at Evan's last statement, wondering if that was possible. But then he remembered the scattered purse. It just couldn't be possible. He was afraid to say anything aloud to Evan. Brandon wondered if he should call the police? What if she got mauled by an animal when she ran back?

Meanwhile, Evan headed back to his truck and reached

into the back seat, pulling out a shotgun. He closed the door and turned around to Brandon.

He looked at the barrel and then back to Brandon. "I never leave home without her," he stated matter-of-factly, noting the look of surprise on Brandon's face.

"Now, tell me where you two headed so we can get moving. This storm is getting closer, and we're losing light quickly."

Brandon pointed toward the path. Without another word, Evan led the way through the woods along the path, as they listened carefully for any sign of life. The wind was whipping through the bare branches now, making a whistling sound as it traveled through the forest. They stopped every minute or so, yelling her name and looking around. The only response they heard was the continued sound of the wind, strengthening with each passing moment.

"Here, this is it. This is where I last saw her," Brandon said, stopping in his footsteps and pointing to the tree where he last saw Maddie. Just a few feet from the fence. Brandon put his fist up to his mouth and held it there, fighting back the urge to cry.

Brandon considered the situation as Evan looked around and then back at him. The spot was remote and far from the road that led to the farm, even farther from the main road. No one would hear him all the way out here if something had happened to them both, he thought to himself.

Evan rubbed the stubble on his chin. "Why did you two come all the way out here? This is quite a ways off the main road, and it can get dangerous during hunting season," he questioned. "You kids are unprepared to be out here like this!"

"I...I just wanted to take Maddie for a small hike to show her around," he lied nervously, hoping it wasn't obvious. He hadn't thought of a good story to tell but needed to come up with something fast. He wasn't ready to admit why he was actually here, not knowing who he could trust and who he couldn't.

Evan surveyed the area one last time before looking Brandon in eye, his shotgun still lazily held in his hand like a lifeless, cold body.

"It's gettin' late, and in about ten minutes we aren't gonna be able to see anything at all. I don't think she'd be dumb enough to cross over this fence this late in the day. I think if I were her, I probably would have headed back to the farm to try to get to a phone."

"I guess so."

Evan made a good point. Maddie knew as much as Brandon did about the area, and that wasn't much at all. The cell reception in this remote area of the world wasn't great, so it was possible that she ran back to the farm.

They turned around and began to head back, Evan leading the way. Brandon kept his eyes trained on the path ahead of them, his shoulders slumped as he contemplated the what-ifs. He quickly shook it off and picked up his pace. Now was the time to focus on getting her back. Dead or alive, he had to find her.

When they reached the road, Brandon stopped and asked Evan, "Do you have a cell that I can use? I don't seem to have good reception out here, but I think I should call the police."

"Sorry," he replied, putting his shotgun back in its place in the truck, "but I don't believe in carrying one of those. Technology seems to have a way of getting people into trouble, and I like to keep my life uncomplicated."

Brandon frantically pulled his phone out of his pocket and looked at the reception bars, walking around in hopes of finding the one spot where at least one bar would appear. After a few minutes of walking around, he finally found a good spot and dialed 9-1-1.

He stumbled through his words as the operator on the other end of the line proceeded with her questions. He watched Evan back at his truck, sitting behind the steering wheel, patiently waiting, one of his legs still hanging out of the open door, casually dangling.

After a few painful minutes of answering questions, the operator updated her notes and placed him on hold to dispatch out to the local barracks. Every minute that passed suddenly began to feel like an eternity, and Brandon felt as though he was beginning to lose his mind with panic.

Brandon's thoughts were interrupted by the sound of sirens in the distance. The operator acknowledged the sound, reminded him to stay calm and try to recount to them exactly what he had transpired, and wished him luck before hanging up the other end of the line. He put the phone back in his pocket and started walking toward the cruiser that had now turned onto Overland Drive.

The cruiser, which carried two officers, came to an abrupt stop on the side of the road, just behind the Jeep. Chief Walker was the first to exit the vehicle out of the driver side as the other officer collected his notepad and pen before trailing behind him.

Chief Walker reached out to shake Brandon's hand before introducing the young detective. "This is Detective Boyland, my right-hand man. I overheard the call come in and wanted to personally come down here with him."

Detective Boyland gave Brandon a firm handshake, tipping his head forward quickly, as if to say hello.

"Now, can you tell me exactly what happened here?"

Brandon quickly explained, "We were driving back to the farm, and I felt a sick feeling in my stomach that seemed to come out of nowhere and had to pull over. I got out of the Jeep with Maddie for some fresh air and decided to walk it off a little bit. The pain got worse, and I found myself unable to walk back, so..." His voice trailed off and he put his hand up to his mouth to muffle the sounds of his quiet sob.

The chief put his hand on Brandon's shoulder and gave it a few gentle squeezes. "It's okay, son. Take all the time you need."

"Thanks, Chief," he replied, taking a deep inhale before continuing on, "She decided to go for help. I sat on the ground and watched her run back toward the direction of the cars, but we were too far back for me to see if she got there. After all this time passed, I just felt something must have happened. That's when I forced myself up and back to the car to find she was gone."

He couldn't control his emotions at this point and let his tears flow wildly. The chief moved in closer to him and rested a hand on his shoulder, giving him a light squeeze.

Detective Boyland stood emotionless, still updating his notes, seemingly unconcerned over her mysterious disappearance. He stood tall, the same height as Brandon. His face was stern, and Brandon could see him biting down in frustration, showing every detail of his square jawline. He sensed Boyland was a hothead, in his late twenties or perhaps early thirties.

Evan, who had exited the truck to quietly listen with curious ears, stood behind Brandon, leaning against the Jeep, ready to offer up his theories when ready.

"Well, she hasn't been gone that long, and it sounds to me like she could have just run back to the farm to get help," Detective Boyland offered.

"Son, have you gone back to the farm to look for her yet?" the chief questioned, in agreement with his partner.

Brandon was confused. He didn't understand why they were so relaxed at this point.

Evan took a step forward from his resting spot and stood beside Brandon.

"I had just come from the farm when I saw Brandon on the side of the road. I mentioned to the boy that I hadn't seen anyone pass and offered to walk out the same path with him to see if we could find her. I think she may be lost in these woods, but we aren't gonna find her now. It's getting late, and there isn't enough light to guide us."

The chief looked around and shook his head.

Brandon could only imagine what he may be thinking. He dropped his shoulders and looked down at his feet. How would they find her this late? Finding someone in the woods during the daylight was hard enough, let alone the darkness. He took a deep breath. He could almost smell the dampness in the air with the impending rainstorm certain to hit in just an hour or so. This would further complicate matters for them.

While the chief continued to survey the area around them, Detective Boyland closed his notebook and looked to Brandon. "I just want to be sure I have this down correctly. You got a headache, pulled over, and decided to venture out in the woods, in unfamiliar territory, right before dark?" he asked, condescendingly.

"Yes, that's exactly what happened."

"Seems to me that you two may have had an argument, no? You sure you aren't leaving anything out?"

"Listen, I know this sounds crazy, but I'm telling you the truth! We didn't argue!" Brandon couldn't contain his anger and began raising his voice. He knew this prick was crossing the line, intentionally trying to rile him. How dare he insinuate that Brandon had anything to do with this!

Chief Walker moved to stand between the two younger men.

"Okay, okay, calm down! Let's not let emotions take over. We need to focus on the facts, and Detective Boyland is doing his job. We need to get back to the station and get a solid plan together. Why don't the two of you follow us back to the office so we can get started?"

Brandon hated the idea of leaving the area for fear Maddie would return to find no one there for her. He shifted back and forth from foot to foot, frantically looking around the woods, while the detectives and Evan began heading back to their vehicles to leave. He didn't want to leave and waste time in an office talking about what to do next. After a few moments, he gave in and reluctantly jumped into his Jeep to follow the other two vehicles back to the barracks, his eyes watching the rearview mirror every few seconds to see if he could catch a glimpse of her running back on the road. It was dusk now, and Brandon knew that once darkness fully engulfed the area, his chances of finding her tonight would be lost.

After a short ride in the world of catastrophic scenarios that ran uncontrollably through his mind, he arrived at the barracks. The other two cars were in front of him and parked in front of the building. Brandon parked across from them and shut off his engine. He exited his Jeep, feeling as though he were watching himself from the outside of his body, hoping that this was some crazy dream.

But this was no dream. This was reality. *His* reality. A nightmare just as cold and bitter as the wind that nipped at his skin.

Chapter Twenty-One

As they entered the barracks, Chief Walker asked both Brandon and Evan to have a seat in the conference room where Brandon and Maddie first met him. Evan excused himself to use the restroom, leaving Brandon alone in the room with his thoughts. He sat at the far end of the room, mindlessly biting his nails, his feet bouncing up and down impatiently under the table. Seconds became minutes, and before he knew it fifteen minutes had passed and no one had come in to speak to him. Just as he began to stand up, Chief Walker came in, Detective Boyland trailing right behind him. The chief quickly explained that they had released Evan just a few moments before and then sat themselves directly across the long conference table to face him.

Chief Walker put his elbows on the table, clasped his hands together in front of his mouth for a moment in silence, then leaned back in the chair, putting his hands back in the familiar spot on his large belly. Tapping them against his uniform just as he did the first time they met.

"I know your girlfriend hasn't been gone that long, but I'm already working to assemble some folks in town to help find her. I'm not gonna sugar coat this for you, son. This is hunting season, and that's gonna add an extra layer of danger to this situation. I've alerted a few key folks to be on the lookout for a lost woman."

The chief turned to Boyland, who looked him in the eye and gave him a slight nod. Then they both turned back to look Brandon directly in the eye before beginning a barrage of questions.

The chief recalled the meeting they had the day before and asked several questions about what had happened in the car, what they had been doing while they were in town, and even details of any conversations they had between each other. Detective Boyland just sat there, staring at Brandon with a scowl.

Brandon answered everything, leaving out all but one detail: the reason they found themselves hiking back in the woods. He didn't feel he could trust them or anyone else in this town with that information.

When the questioning finally seemed to be over, Detective Boyland sat forward in his chair, crossing his arms on the table in front of him. The cold stare never left his face.

"You know? I used to hear stories like this all the time when I was an officer in the city. The girlfriend disappears and the boyfriend has no idea where she is. The boyfriend seems to cooperate with us but leaves out one key detail in his statement."

Brandon swallowed as quietly as he could, a cold sweat breaking out on his head. The walls of the conference room closed in on him as Boyland continued his theory.

"The boyfriend forgets to tell us about the argument that they had hours or even days before. The girlfriend finds herself in a secluded area with the boyfriend. They continue to argue outside, only the boyfriend becomes enraged and strangles the girl, unable to control his emotions. After he realizes what he has done, he needs a way to get rid of the body and hides her body where he thinks no one can find her."

Brandon stood up so fast from his seat that the chair went flying back and nearly hit the wall behind him. "Are you implying that I killed Maddie and am trying to cover it up?"

"I'm saying I know that you are hiding something from us. I can see it in your eyes."

The detective sat back smugly in his chair with his cold stare. Brandon looked back to the chief.

"I'm begging you to help me." Tears welled up in his eyes. "I love Maddie and I just want to bring her back. I want this nightmare to be over, and I'm asking for your help. I swear I didn't have anything to do with her vanishing, other than making the mistake of letting her leave my side." He stood there searching the chief's eyes for anything. He couldn't believe that they would think he could have something to do with this.

The chief contemplated for a few moments, looking at the detective and then back to Brandon. He stood up, and both he and Boyland moved to stand next to the door. Brandon looked at both of them. Time was ticking and every minute seemed like an eternity to him.

"Gentlemen, I think this is a conversation best had *after* we find the young lady. The fact is we need to locate her and bring her back to safety before we deal with the specifics."

The chief calmly explained the plan he had formulated to try and find her. They would alert the other troopers at the station and could mobilize other volunteers in town to help look for Maddie the next morning.

Brandon's heart sank. He couldn't bear thinking of her in the woods for one more minute, let alone a full night.

The chief looked to Brandon with determination. "I will give you my word that I will help to bring this town together to bring her home."

Brandon nodded his head to the detective as a *thanks-for-nothing* move, before moving to shake the chief's hand goodbye. He left the building, heart in hand, to make the trip back to the farm in silence.

Back inside the barracks, Detective Boylan and Chief Walker watched from the conference room window, as Brandon left the parking lot.

"He's holding something back, Andrew. I can see it in his eyes." Without waiting for a response from the chief, he left the room.

The chief stared out the window and whispered, "I know he is too."

Chapter Twenty-Two

On the way home from the barracks, Brandon made a desperate call back home to Jimmy. He picked up right away.

Before Brandon could utter a single word, Jimmy blurted out, "Brandon, I heard. I'm so sorry!" Evan had been by not long before to drop off supplies and had informed Jimmy of what happened. "She still isn't home, but don't worry, son, we are going to find her."

"Thanks, Dad. I'll be home in a few minutes and I'm coming over. I need your help with our own plan. The police want to wait until tomorrow, but something has to be done tonight." And with that, he hung up and raced out of the parking lot, heading back home.

A few minutes later, the tires of his Jeep came to a screeching halt in front of his grandma's house. He looked across the lawn to the cabin with a small sliver of hope that she would be there with a light on, but the house was dark and empty.

He ran up the front porch steps, pushed the door to his

grandma's house open, and ran inside to find Jimmy right there behind the door waiting to embrace him. He grabbed on to him tightly, burying his head in his shoulder and sobbing almost uncontrollably. Jimmy stood with him in the foyer, holding his son, reassuring him that he would do what he could to help bring her back. Any ill feelings the two had felt just a day before were forgotten in that moment. Brandon needed Jimmy now more than ever and convinced himself there was no way this man could have done anything to harm her. He *had* to believe that or they would never find her. He needed someone on his side who could help him, and Jimmy could be counted on to do just that. The two men went over to the couch in the living room and immediately got down to business.

"Okay, let's start from the beginning. Give me all the details. I need to know what the two of you were doing, what the police asked you, what you saw around you when you noticed she was missing...everything."

Brandon explained what had happened just as he did an hour before down in the conference room at the barracks. He felt as though he were on autopilot. His words disconnected from his thoughts, which were solely focused on Madeline. He just spit out what he could like a tape recording being played back.

After Brandon finished giving him every detail, Jimmy took it in for a moment, sitting back in the chair and rubbing his chin in thought. The faint scratching sound from the stubble on his face was the only sound filling the room as his hand moved back and forth. He leaned forward and looked Brandon in the eye. "What were you two doing out in that section of the farm?" He looked confused.

"I just needed to walk off the feeling of nausea...I dunno. We weren't really thinking about where we were going, we were just moving. The next thing you know, we were in the middle of the woods." Even Brandon was convincing himself of the story he had weaved to cover up the true purpose of the walk.

Jimmy continued to ask questions, and Brandon answered him with as much detail as he felt was needed to aid in the search, paying little attention to whatever advice Jimmy offered in between answers and questions. In his mind, he was formulating a plan to find her on his own. Jimmy alluded to the fact that morning was the best time to search. The woods were dark, and they would never find her tonight. But Brandon wouldn't accept that. He *couldn't* accept that.

"Don't try to solve this on your own, Bran," he warned, as if he were reading Brandon's thoughts. "You know nothing about this farm or the people in this town."

"I can't just sit here and do nothing! Maddie needs me and I have to find her, goddammit!" he snapped back, instantly feeling guilty for lashing out.

"I get it, son, but you won't be doing her any favors if you go out in the dark and get lost yourself! You need to be realistic. There are things we can do right now without venturing out into the woods." He stood up and pulled out his phone to look through pictures. "Let's start by finding a recent picture of her so we can quickly make some fliers in the office." His thumb began moving up and down the screen in search of the right one.

Brandon rolled his eyes while Jimmy's attention was on his phone. He didn't understand why no one wanted to physically look for her in the dark; it could be done with the right lights, he thought. Feeling as though he had little choice in the matter, he pulled his phone out of his pocket and also began to look for pictures at Jimmy's suggestion. It didn't take him long to find one that he felt was best through the many pictures he had of her. He took a moment to take in her face. She was standing out by the side of the road overlooking the city skyline during a trip they had taken down to Manhattan last spring. Brandon remembered it like it had just happened yesterday. Her face was filled with excitement that day as they prepared to see their first Broadway show, *Hamilton.* They saved for months to score the tickets and made a day of it. They dined together at the Boathouse in Central Park, grabbed coffee at a local shop in Little Italy, and finally took in the evening show before crashing in a hotel nearby. It was the perfect day, and her smile was all the proof he needed.

"Here." He got up and walked over to Jimmy, turning the phone to show him. "I think this one is best."

Jimmy took the phone and quickly walked to the den. The den was a small room just off the kitchen, lined with bookshelves. In the middle of the room was an antique desk with a leather top where Grandma Alice used to conduct the business on the farm or write letters to friends and family. There was a large window facing the back of the house with a view of the pond. An old brown leather rocker was situated next to it where Brandon could recall sitting in his grandma's lap as a child, reading books almost every night. Jimmy took a seat at the desk and opened up his laptop to begin working on a flier. Brandon walked around to where Jimmy sat and kneeled down beside him.

Jimmy typed out the word "MISSING" in bright red font at the top of the page.

Brandon felt as though he had been punched in the gut over and over as the fact of her disappearance became more of a reality with each detail spelled out on the screen. Jimmy uploaded the picture of her and pasted it on the document before printing it out to review. They both stood and walked over to the printer, listening as the machine moved its lasers back and forth, back and forth, before finally spitting out the first copy of Maddie's poster.

Jimmy looked at his watch. "We can start by taking copies of these down the road to Vinny's. It is the tail end of dinnertime, but I'm sure there are still folks sitting at the bar."

Brandon stood next to him with the paper in hand, frozen. Jimmy put his hand on his shoulder and gave him a gentle squeeze. He knew what it was like to feel the pain and fear of losing someone and not knowing what had happened to them.

"The best thing we can do for Maddie right now is keep the faith. Don't give up like I did, kid."

He pulled his son in for a quick embrace before walking out of the den to get his coat and keys. Brandon followed behind him, lost in a maelstrom of emotions. In his heart, he felt it was too late to try and put up signs that no one would see at night, but he had nothing to lose. He quickly turned around and headed back to the office to a couple of sheets of paper and pen to write notes for Maddie to call his cell in case she came to the house. He ran back out and taped it to the front door before joining Jimmy in the truck to go to Vinny's.

"Can you stop by the cabin really quick?"

"Sure thing, son."

Just a few seconds later, Brandon ran up the steps to the cabin, opened the door, and flipped on the lights. Foolishly, he hoped she would come out of the bedroom to surprise him there. But the cabin was empty, not a sound to penetrate the stillness of the air around him.

Brandon taped the second copy of his note to Maddie on the front of the cabin door and walked back out to head to town.

Chapter Twenty-Three

Several minutes later, Brandon and Jimmy came to a screeching halt in the dirt lot of Vinny's. Brandon glanced at his watch. It was just past seven in the evening, and the restaurant was still open, with a few cars parked outside. The two of them ran inside and stopped in the entranceway, glancing around for the best place to start. There were four people at the bar, a couple at one end and two other gentlemen who sat by themselves at other stools. A small family sat in the corner across from the bar in the restaurant area. Jimmy took the stack of fliers from Brandon's hands and led them to the bar where the couple sat.

"Sorry to bother you," Brandon interrupted, as Jimmy slid one of the fliers next to the lady's beer.

The two of them stopped their conversation and turned to them with polite smiles.

"My name is Brandon Stone," he said, offering them both his hand before introducing them to Jimmy, who did the same. "My family owns the farm just up the road."

Brandon briefly put his fist up to his mouth before

continuing on, fighting the urge to let his emotion take over. Jimmy put his hand on his shoulder and squeezed.

Taking a deep breath in, he continued, "My girlfriend went missing earlier this afternoon...this is her." He pointed toward the flier, then went on to briefly explain where she went missing and that they were looking to have anyone in town help.

The woman, older with a short, gray bob and brown eyes, replied first, "I'm so sorry!" She picked the flier up and studied it carefully. She introduced herself as May and leaned back a bit to introduce them to her husband, Paul, who had the same gray-colored hair as his wife. "We live just a few miles down the road here as well, and we know the farm." She tore a piece of paper off the bottom of the flier and searched through the purse that hung from her chair for a pen. She quickly wrote her name and number and invited them to call her and Paul if they needed help "in the morning."

They turned back to each other and resumed drinking the libations set before them. To Brandon, it appeared much easier for them to remove themselves from his reality than it was to share in the pain.

In the morning.

He was sick of hearing that phrase. Brandon still couldn't wrap his head around the thought that no one would help him tonight. But he followed Jimmy's silent cue, and they turned to speak to the other two gentlemen at the opposite end of the bar.

Both gentlemen were dressed in flannel and quietly enjoying their beers. They did not seem to be there together, as there were two seats in between them that sat empty. The larger gentleman sported a bushy beard and a Carhartt knit cap. The scrawnier man was clean cut, though both of them appeared to be hunters. Hunters seemed to have a more distinct look than most, and Brandon noted that most of them wore the same type of flannel shirts and heavy utility jackets, with pockets that looked deep enough to carry just about everything except a shotgun.

After briefly introducing themselves, Brandon laid the fliers down on the bar, placing separate ones in front of each of them. They both quickly looked before the larger man to his left spoke.

"I didn't see anything out of the ordinary today, but we've been out hunting all day, so we stay pretty disconnected from the world around us." He introduced himself as Tom and offered up his big, burly hand to both of them.

Despite sitting a couple of bar stools apart, the men knew each other. Tom introduced the scrawnier of the pair as Joe. Neither of them lived in the area full-time but owned a piece of land to hunt and fish on throughout the year. Thanksgiving week was a popular week for hunting.

Scrawny Joe spent more time studying his flier. Brandon caught him in the corner of his eye brushing a thumb over Maddie's cheek in the picture. Brandon suddenly felt uneasy.

"I don't know many folks in the area, but I know I would remember a face like that if I saw it," he said, never removing his eyes from the flier in his hands. "She's a beauty, that's for sure. Reminds me of my own daughter."

His consolation didn't make Brandon feel any more at ease, and his frustration was brewing as he watched Joe continue to examine the flier and picture in great detail.

He placed the flier down and finally turned to meet eyes with Brandon and Jimmy. "I'm sure you'll find her soon. We'll be sure to keep an extra eye out for the little lady, won't we, Joe?"

"Yeah, we'll keep an eye."

Something just didn't sit right with these two, Brandon thought. But he dismissed the feeling and politely shook both their hands. He and Jimmy turned around to see who else they could speak to when Violet emerged from the back with two hot plates of food in her hands. She smiled at them briefly and said hello, before quickly passing them to deliver the food to May and Paul. A few moments later, she came over to the spot where they stood and asked if she could get them anything.

Brandon handed her the flier. She picked it up, and her hand immediately flew to cover her mouth as she gasped.

"No! Please tell me this is not what I think it is!" she asked in a voice an octave higher than it normally was. "What happened?" Her hand slowly came back down to the paper flier, holding it with both hands.

"It happened just after we saw you this morning at the cemetery," he replied. He was beginning to feel like he was looking from the outside in. He no longer felt connected with his body, listening to his own story. But he continued to explain to her what had happened. "Next thing I know, she's gone. Listen, Violet, I need you to be honest here"—he swallowed nervously—"do you think Chad could have something to do with this?"

Chad had been on his mind since they walked to the bar. He remembered the story she had told him regarding their brief friendship, if that's what it was called, back in the day with his mother.

"Chad Zewlinski?" Her face showed disbelief. "I don't think so, Brandon. He wouldn't have any reason to get involved in your life, in my opinion. I mean, other than the brief friendship with your mother, he just keeps to himself and doesn't seem to bother anyone or even care to engage with another human being. And his obvious crush on her seemed mostly innocent. I can't imagine him wanting to stir up trouble."

Brandon forced a small smile on his face and shook her hand. "No one knows the folks around here like you do, Violet." He handed her a stack of the fliers. "If it's not too much to ask, can you just hand these out to whomever comes in? It would mean a lot to me."

She nodded in agreement and tucked the papers under her arm, using her free arm to reach up and hug him before doing the same to Jimmy.

"We'll find her, honey, don't worry. Tomorrow is a new day."

Tomorrow. Brandon repeated that word in his head. *Tomorrow it will be too late.*

Chapter Twenty-Four

The pair of them walked to the car in silence, each thinking of what to do next. Brandon wasn't convinced that Chad was so innocent. People could get comfortable with a person and miss out on clues. Or even worse, just blissfully ignore wrongdoings. Chad knew something, Brandon felt it. He needed to go under the radar and search his property somehow, and since no one could help him tonight, he would help himself by formulating a plan to do just that.

Jimmy drove them back to the farm, uttering words of support here and there. Brandon could hear him, but nothing comforted him. When they arrived, Jimmy offered to have Brandon stay at the main house with him, but Brandon insisted on staying in the cabin.

"It's going to be okay. You hear me? We WILL find her," he reassured Brandon. Jimmy gave him a tight hug and then held his shoulders and looked Brandon in the eyes with determination.

"Thanks, Dad. We'd better get some rest so we can start again tomorrow. I'll be here at 7 a.m., okay?"

He turned and walked back to the cabin using his phone camera to illuminate the path. Jimmy stood watching him until Brandon made it to the porch and turned to wave goodbye.

Brandon walked into the empty cabin and hung his coat up before taking a seat on the sofa. He sat down on the couch and rested his forehead in his hands. He sat there for an hour in heavy thought before deciding it was best to get to bed. He turned off all the lights except for the light in the living room and retired to the bedroom. As he lay in bed, he began to pray, *God, please. If you're listening, please help me. Help me find Maddie.*

He heard nothing except the sound of his heart. An emptiness filled the room as he let the hope of finding her alive begin to slip away with each passing second.

Brandon hastily sat up and grabbed the phone next to the bed. 6:14 in the morning. Thanksgiving was tomorrow and it didn't feel that way to him. If he couldn't find her, there would be nothing left in this town for him. Nothing to be thankful for. He ran his fingers through his hair and looked around the room to find all was still the same as it was last night. He quickly got up and went to the bathroom to splash water on his face before running into the living room to look out the front door window. It was still somewhat dark, and the moon was covered by the clouds above, but he could see the soft purple and deep red colors of the sun behind the bare trees beginning to rise.

Disappointed, he turned around and looked at himself in the mirror by the front door. Dark circles around his eyes from restless sleep and stress were beginning to set in, and he felt like he was falling apart. Although the sun hadn't fully risen yet, Brandon decided he needed to get going. It would be up soon enough, and he didn't want to waste any of it sitting in this cabin. He changed into jeans and a flannel, hastily brushed his teeth, grabbed his phone and his keys, and planned to drive to Chad's house. Without thinking, he stopped in the living room and glanced around in thought. *Maybe this isn't such a good idea*, he mulled. Slowly, he walked over to the sofa and sat down, taking in a calming breath, letting go of the adrenaline and letting his body settle for the moment.

He saw himself as a child on the floor in front of the fire-place, playing with his toys, his mom bustling around the house cleaning. At that moment, his heart filled with love and loss. He mourned for his mother, and yet somehow, he also felt the joy he must have felt at that moment in time, the feeling of safety enveloping him like a warm blanket. Brandon's eyes tracked above the fireplace to the old mirror. Half the size of the mantle and framed in an ornate silver frame, it was the focal point of the room. All of a sudden, it dawned on him...it wasn't *just* a mirror.

Brandon remembered watching his mom open the mirror like a door, as he used to play in the middle of the room. She would place things in there or take them out. One day, Brandon gave her his toy telephone for her to put in there. He remembered her taking it, a smile on her face, and placing it in the special cubby behind the mirror above the fireplace. She closed the door to the mirror, then put her finger to her mouth and winked, like she was signaling to the then two-year-old Brandon that this was their special hiding spot. "Shhhhhhh..." she breathed with a smile.

Snapping back from his memory, his heart began to race in anticipation. He moved quickly to the mirror and carefully pulled on the right side, noting the hinges were still on the left-hand side, just as he remembered. And there, behind the same mirror that hung for years, was a small, hidden door to the secret storage space. He placed his fingers behind the groove of the small door to pull it back and reveal what was left inside.

Tears welled up in his eyes as he peered inside. He wondered if his mom's hands were the last to touch the secret space. He wondered if anyone else knew it was even there or if it was just a secret kept locked up inside this house that only he and his mother shared.

Inside, he saw the old play phone, with its happy eyes and friendly smile, just as he remembered. He pulled the phone out and gently ran his thumb along the receiver. He placed it on the mantle and looked around the room to make sure no one was watching. Looking back inside, he found a Smith and Wesson 10mm gun. He slowly took the gun out, examining it with a delicate eye. Though the gun was empty of bullets, there in the safe was also a box of bullets and an envelope full of cash. Brandon didn't take the time to count it out, but it appeared to be a couple thousand. He took the cash out of the envelope and shoved it in his front pocket. Looking around, he grabbed bullets from the box and loaded the gun, placing a few extra in his pocket opposite the cash. Picking the gun up off the mantle once more, he tucked it in the back of the waistband in his jeans, pulling his flannel shirt over it, his palms sweaty and his pulse racing like a horse.

Brandon put back the empty envelope and his toy phone, closing the door to the hidden safe and tucking it all away behind the old mirror. Taking the sleeve of his flannel and bringing it down around his palm, he cleaned up any evidence left behind of his fingerprints before turning around to head out the front door.

He texted Jimmy while walking:

Hey, Dad, I can't sit here and wait. I need to go out and find her. Can you please follow up with the detective this morning?

Zwoop! Off his message went in hopes that he wasn't awake to text back. Brandon didn't want to deal with questions from Jimmy right now, and he purposely didn't tell Jimmy where he was going. He couldn't afford to put him in danger as well. He shoved the phone in his pocket, got in the Jeep, and sped down the driveway toward Chad's property.

When Chad's mailbox was in view, Brandon slowed the Jeep down a bit. He passed the mailbox and the empty driveway and looked around for a place where he could discreetly store his Jeep and walk undetected through the wooded area. He pulled off the side of the road just a quarter mile from his target and carefully navigated the Jeep through the slightly rugged terrain of the woods and out of sight of the road. He cut the engine and stepped out, tracing his steps back the way he came to make sure they were less noticeable.

No one was around. The air was calm and silent with only the crunching of the leaves underneath his boots making any sound. Tiny beads of sweat were forming on his brow despite the chill in the air as the adrenaline pumped through his body like a machine. He could see the back of Chad's shed in view in the distance, just at the edge of his property. The driveway that led to Chad's house was void of any vehicles, giving Brandon a small sense of relief. He quickened his pace and arrived at the back of the shed, crouching down low behind it, as he surveyed the area around him to make sure he was still alone.

He walked around to the front of the shed and peeked into one of the picture windows on the front to examine the inside. On one side were shelves packed neatly with boxes. The rest of the shed consisted of lawn tools, neatly hung on peg boards, and a large, ride-on mower was parked in the middle of it all. The door to the shed had a sliding lock but no deadbolt. He slid the lock to the right and pulled back the handle. He entered the shed with his back first, watching Chad's property in front of him as he slowly pulled the shed door closed.

Once inside, he walked to the wall with boxes and took his finger to carefully lift up each lid of the old filing type boxes to reveal their contents. The boxes had white labels on the front marked in black marker. Most boxes were filled with old journals and some labeled as taxes. The contents inside the boxes he checked were neatly organized with file folders. He stood back to look at the bottom shelf and noted that one of the labels said "MISC" in all-cap black letters.

He kneeled down and pulled the box off of the shelf, blew the dust off the top, and opened it up.

On top was a neatly folded pink and purple flannel top. Underneath he found what appeared to be a journal, and some other knickknacks. He pulled the journal out. "2004" was all that the label said on the front. His heart sank before he even opened it. The year his mom had disappeared.

Opening the cover, he began to skim through the entries, looking for anything obvious. There was a small break in the middle of the book. He opened the section up, and a picture fell into his lap.

A picture of Ella.

Brandon felt his heart pound as if it were outside of his chest, and his ears rang like the sound of a tuning fork, drowning out other sounds. This was the *same* picture he had held on to in the red tin box next to his bed for the last twenty years of his life, but it had been altered. Instead of seeing his dad next to his mom, he saw Chad's face glued over his dad's body. Nausea began to settle in as he looked in disbelief. Placing the picture down next to him, he returned his attention back to the page where he'd found it to read the passage.

I'm in love with a woman in town. A black-haired beauty who has a smile fit for an angel. I can't believe I've known her for so long, yet somehow, it's like I'm seeing and hearing her for the first time. She married that prick of a man, Jimmy, but I can tell just from talking to her, she's not in love with him. I've been watching her for months, and her sadness pains me so much, I just want to comfort her. But I haven't had the courage to say a word. But tonight, oh my God, tonight...I did! Maybe it was the whiskey, maybe the air in the bar, who knows? But I fucking did it! I spoke to her! She didn't seem to remember me from high school, but I didn't care. There was this energy between us, I could feel it! And I made her smile. Oh, that smile! I'll go slow, Ella, I promise. Friends first, marriage later. This is the one. I just need to show her what we can be. Somehow, someway, I'll show her.

Brandon continued reading as much as his stomach would allow. The obsession that Chad had over his mother was both repulsive and frightening. Chad described her in intimate detail in the pages that followed. What clothes she wore, how she ate, even her time with Brandon. There were logs of her whereabouts scratched onto pages in the margins as he followed her every move.

Oh my God! He was sitting in the woods watching her at the house! Brandon couldn't believe what he was seeing. He described in detail the cabin, her bedtime routine, and even what time she arose in the mornings. Chad recounted how he would "casually" show up at places he'd knew she'd be, and laughed to himself knowing she was unaware he was with her. Always.

Brandon continued to skim through the other two journals to see if anything else stood out. And that's when the entries began to turn dark. His mom must have picked up on the obsession at some point. The last entry was dated November 21, 2004, a day before his mom went missing forever.

For months I've been working on Ella, and the bitch won't budge! I can't take this anymore! Just another fucking whore, toying with me like I'm a fucking pet! If it weren't for that prick of a husband, she could have been mine, I just know it! No, no! I can't think like that...I need to relax. She's not like the others...I can't believe this. I just need her to see we were meant to be together. I told her I need to see her again tomorrow, just one last time. I have to confess my love to her. She thinks I'm overpowering our friendship, but she doesn't see! We are meant for one another!

Suddenly, Brandon could hear a vehicle in the distance. He held his breath for a moment to see if the vehicle would continue on, but a few seconds later he heard the tires make their connection with the shale on Chad's driveway, like eggs frying in a pan.

Shit! He quickly threw the contents back into the box and shoved it back on the shelf where he found it, keeping the picture of his mother, which he shoved into his back pocket. Raising himself to his knees, he peered out the front window. Chad's truck was parked now, but Chad was nowhere to be seen.

Keeping his body low, he crawled over to the front door and gently pushed it open to peek outside. When he felt he was somewhat safe, he crawled out the front door, standing up to a crouch as he pushed the door closed behind him. Silence.

He carefully slid the lock on the door back into its hole, his back to the driveway. As he turned around to run back to the woods, he stopped short, jumping back in shock. *Chad!*

Chad stood there with the scowl of an angered, crazy man. Knife in hand, ready to kill.

Chapter Twenty-Five

"What the fuck are you doing here?" he screamed, knife still slightly above his head, like a snake in strike formation. He took a step closer to Brandon. He could feel his breath, hot on his face.

Brandon stood his ground. "Tell me where Madeline is, you sick son of a bitch!"

"I don't know anything about your friend, kid..." He moved another inch closer to Brandon's face. "...All I know is you are trespassing on private property...MY PROPERTY...and I want you gone!"

Without so much as a blink, Brandon pulled the picture out of his back pocket and thrust it in front of Chad's face. "I know you took her! And I know you had something to do with my mother too! ADMIT IT, you fucking bastard! You took them both from me!"

Chad snatched the picture from Brandon's hand and looked at it briefly before throwing it on the ground and spitting on it. "You think you know, but you don't. You know *nothing* about me or her. You can't just come here and root through my belongings! You think I give a shit about your mother anymore? Or your stupid girlfriend?" He smirked as he backed away, lowering the knife down to his side. "You know what I think? I think your mom got what she deserved. And your girl? She probably smartened up and left your ass. I think you need to leave. NOW!"

Brandon heeded his word, backing away slowly at first, his eyes locked with Chad's. Once he got another foot past the front of the shed where he had a clear view of the woods from where he came, he turned and ran back to the Jeep, tearing out of the woods and back onto the road with less care than he had when he came in. Chad stood in his driveway watching, right where Brandon left him.

A few minutes later, he pulled up the roundabout in front of his grandmother's house. The lights were on in the living room, and Jimmy's truck was parked at the side of the house. Brandon ran up the stairs to the porch and flew inside without knocking or warning his stepfather of his arrival.

Jimmy jumped up out of his seat in the living room and ran to Brandon, giving him a hug. "Where were you, Bran?" he asked, clearly worried that he had vanished as well. "I tried calling you a million times, son. Don't just leave without telling me!"

"I had to try and find her, Dad. I barely slept last night. She's out there somewhere!" His voice reflected his panic.

"Brandon, I know this is hard. Trust me, I know. But we need to let the police do their job. We don't know who is out there and if they're waiting for you too. I can't lose you too, you hear me?"

"I—" Brandon stopped short as he saw a pair of headlights headed down the driveway toward the house. His heart sank for a moment. It was a trooper SUV. Brandon feared the worst as he ran outside and down the stairs to meet them.

The SUV stopped behind Brandon's Jeep, and the door opened for him to see it was Chief Walker.

"Afternoon, Brandon, Jimmy," he said, tipping his hat forward to them both. "I'm afraid I don't have any news for you, but I do have to show you this." He pulled a plastic bag out from his car and walked over to where Brandon and Jimmy where standing.

Brandon felt the blood draining out of his face and he immediately felt weak. He could see the brown boot that she was just wearing yesterday when he last saw her. It had stains on it, but he couldn't tell if it was blood or dirt. *No!* His throat felt as it were closing in on itself, and he struggled to breathe.

"Take a deep breath, Brandon," Jimmy said, rubbing his back gently.

"We've been working all morning to survey the area. We found this in a ditch just up Highway 6, about three miles from here. We found this there. I'm guessing by the look on your face, this must belong to her."

Brandon could only manage to nod his head.

The chief went on to explain that they found nothing else in the area. They had spoken to just about everyone in town, and no one seemed to know anything. The troopers had set up checkpoints at strategic areas around town so that anyone coming in or out could be questioned.

Brandon stood in disbelief. He felt as though someone were holding his head underwater. He could hear the chief speaking, but the words became muffled, and little black dots formed in his eyes before he stumbled forward, throwing his arms out on the SUV to brace himself.

"Chief, I think we should get this boy inside. Why don't you come on in so we can sit him down."

The three men went inside and sat Brandon down at the couch in front of the coffee table in the living area. Jimmy ran off to the kitchen and returned a few minutes with a glass of water. He put it in front of Brandon and motioned for Chief to come and talk to him in the corner, lowering their voices so Brandon wouldn't be able to hear them speak.

Brandon sat motionless on the couch, his eyes trained on the glass of water in front of him. *Please, God! Wake me up. Please wake me up.* He squeezed his eyes shut for a moment and then opened them.

Nothing changed.

Chief Walker walked back over to where Brandon sat and told him he would keep searching before he shook their hands goodbye. Jimmy led the chief to the door, mumbling some more before opening the door to let him out.

Jimmy came back and offered to make him some lunch, but Brandon wasn't in the mood to eat. He walked off to make them both some coffee, and Brandon began to form a new plan in his mind.

He needed to get to that field again where this all began. And he needed to get back there alone.

"Dad," he called back to the kitchen where Jimmy was preparing the coffee, "I'll be back. I need to go out and walk around. I'll just be a little bit, and I won't leave the property, okay?"

And without waiting for a response, he was out the door and running down the driveway toward Overland Drive to find the path where this nightmare began.

Chapter Twenty-Six

Maddie's eyes began to flutter open under the cloth that covered her eyes, her head pounding from the blow she took to the side of her head. She tried to remember what had happened, but her mind was still foggy. She could see out through the cloth from a small opening just below her left eye to see the dried blood on the front of her cashmere sweater. Her pulse quickened and her breath intensified, but no sound would escape, as her mouth had been gagged. Her hope began fading. Even if she could manage a scream, she feared no one would hear her, wherever she was. She sensed that she was inside some type of room, as she carefully rubbed her lone bare foot along some type of woven material. The air smelled dank and felt frigid.

With her breath becoming more steady, she listened intently for signs of her captor, but all was silent. She began fumbling at the rope that bound her hands together behind her back.

"Careful there, young lady. Wouldn't want you to ruin

the party, now, would we?" a voice spoke from behind her in the corner.

Maddie froze. She could hear her captor walk toward her from behind, stopping just behind her, his legs barely touching the tips of her fingers.

He leaned in toward her right ear. "You gonna be a good girl if I take off your blindfold?"

She nervously nodded her head. He walked around to the front of the chair and slowly lifted the cloth from her eyes. She stared down at his brown work boots, afraid to face him yet, though she knew who he was the minute his deep, raspy voice penetrated the room.

He put his hand under her chin and lifted it up to look her in the eye. Evan. Tears flowed from her eyes.

"Come on now, darlin'," he said, one side of his mouth forming an evil-looking smile, "don't tell me you didn't see this coming."

He caressed the side of her face with the back of his cold, rough hand and then carefully removed her gag.

"Why are you doin—"

His fingers flew to her mouth and cut her off. "Shhhh, don't say a word or I'll kill you," he warned, matter-of-factly.

Evan grabbed himself and began rubbing around the front of his jeans, never removing his eyes from hers. Maddie tried to wriggle her hands free from the rope behind the chair unsuccessfully.

"Don't try to fight your way out of this one. The way I see it, I'm in control here, and I can end your life in just one move if you give me any trouble."

He leaned in to her face, and his tongue licked her pursed lips.

Maddie quickly turned her face away from him as he tried to pry her mouth open. He grabbed her by the chin and forced her head back to face him.

Maddie spit at his face. Stunned, he stood up and wiped the spit from his cheek, examining his wet fingers as if he had just been stung by a bee.

His angered gaze turned to her and *slap!* The force from his hand was so strong, it sent blood flying out of her mouth and onto the floor. She turned to him and looked him straight in the eye, anger boiling within her, and she spit a mouth full of blood at his feet in defiance. His fist came down to her head with a blow, knocking her and the chair to the floor with a thud.

The pain quickly branched out through her entire head, the familiar little dots coming into view. He kicked her again. And then once more, finally sending her back into unconsciousness.

Chapter Twenty-Seven

Brandon felt the cold water pelt his face, as the first of the freezing rain droplets began falling from the sky. His pace was steady as he continued running toward the path. With each moment, the rain became stronger and stronger, drowning out any sounds from the woods around him.

He reached the path and stopped for a moment to get his breath. The familiar headache settled in, once he reached the same spot. Letting the intensity of the pain guide him, he carefully started jogging back into the brush. The rain pushed the leaves down into the path, making it difficult to follow the exact route back to the wooded fence where he last saw Maddie. Brandon made it past the tree where he last saw her and continued for a few more minutes before reaching the wood fence. Pausing for only a moment, he jumped the fence and ran out to the edge of the clearing before stopping once again.

Looking around at the vast field and the trees surrounding him, he knew he'd been in this very spot before. Brandon's heart was beating outside of his chest now and through his ears. *This is the field from my dreams!*

He ran as fast as he could through the middle of the field, the wind howling and pushing the rain sideways. And that's when he saw it. The roof of the shed. He picked up his pace to a sprint, his boots thumping the ground louder than the pelting rain around him.

"Maddie!" he screamed as he got closer to the shed. "Maddie!"

He slowed his pace as he reached the end of the field and back into the forest on the opposite end of where he began, mere feet from the familiar shed. He peered through the window at the front of the shed. It was just as he had dreamt! The table in the middle of the room. The chair. The shovels in the corner. It was all there! He quickly shifted to the front door and reached up above the frame to find the key when he felt the sharp blow to the back of his head, which sent him flying face-first into the closed door and onto the ground with a loud thud.

His mind went black.

Chapter Twenty-Eight

Brandon found himself sitting in the middle of the field, his head pounding with extreme pain. The rain came down in sheets all around him. He put his fingers gently to the back of his head where the pain seemed to radiate the most. Pulling his hands in front of him, he saw the blood dripping from his hands as the rain washed it onto the ground in front of him, staining the dead grass crimson where he sat.

His head began to feel dizzy, the earth beneath him felt as though it were shifting, and the field began to spin. He quickly stood up and began taking deep breaths to fend off the vomit forming in the pit of his stomach. *Maddie!* He saw the shed in the distance and began to run back toward it, unaware of why he was back in the middle of the field again. He looked all around as he reached the front of the shed again, but no one seemed to be around. Brandon slowly made his way around the shed, keeping his back up against the wood frame.

When he reached the back of the shed, he froze.

A man stood just feet from where Brandon was with his back to him. He wore a green slicker with the hood up over his head. In front of him was Maddie, lying lifeless against a tree. Her head slumped over, her red hair covered in mud and wet with rain was slightly covering the front of her face. The man reached down, putting his hand on her chin, moving her head up to reveal the side of her face.

Brandon gasped. Maddie's face was swollen and covered in bruises and dried blood. Suddenly, her right eye popped open to stare at her captor, her left eye too swollen to follow suit.

She's alive!

The man continued to hold her face, and both he and Maddie seemed to be frozen in time.

Brandon took a few steps toward them and quietly picked up a large, dead branch from the ground. He took the slimmer end in both hands and carefully raised it above his head. His arms locked, and he stood there frozen with them, unable to move. He tried to scream, but no sound emerged from his lips.

As if someone had hit the play button on a remote, the man's hand dropped from Maddie's face, leaving just her and Brandon motionless, and he pulled the hood down from his head. Slowly turning toward Brandon with a sly smile on his face, his eyes locked with Brandon.

Chad!

Chapter Twenty-Nine

Brandon awoke to cold water being thrown on his face. His head throbbed with pain where he had been hit. *Another fucking dream!*

He was inside what he believed to be the shed. He could hear the rain pelting the metal roof above him. His hands were tied behind him, his eyes covered and mouth held tightly by a thick piece of fabric. He tried to move his fingers to the back of his pants to feel for his gun, but it was gone.

"Looking for something?" a voice said from directly behind him, the cool metal of the pistol pushing into the back of his head just below where he had been hit.

Brandon tried to compute the sound of the voice he was hearing, but his ears were still ringing. He attempted to scream, the sounds muffled by the gag in his mouth.

"Don't waste your breath, son. No one will hear from here, trust me on that," warned the man now speaking directly into Brandon's right ear, the heat from his breath penetrating Brandon's neck. He walked around to stand directly in front of Brandon just as he had done hours before with Madeline. "I have no idea how you managed to find this place out here. Not even those idiot troopers could find this place, not that they cared to even look that hard. Not surprised, though. Your mom was smart like that, too. Too smart, in fact, which is why I had to kill her."

Brandon's breath stopped for a moment in shock, and his ears stopped ringing before he realized the error in his dream. This wasn't Chad...this was Evan. His fear was confirmed when Evan removed the blindfold from his eyes to reveal his worn skin and sick smile.

Evan backed up against the wall and casually bent one knee up to rest his foot on the wood panels. He examined the pistol he had taken from Brandon in his hand, as if trying to see his own reflection in the steel as he moved it back and forth. He pushed himself off the wall and walked over to the table next to where Brandon sat. He sat down on the top of it and placed the gun next to him.

His gaze shifted out the window just behind him, a cold smile plastered on his face like the Joker just before he spoke again.

"Hunting is a beautiful sport. I've spent a lifetime doing it, but it wasn't until just before you were born that I realized just how satisfying it could really be. You see"—he turned back to face Brandon now, whose face had frozen in disbelief—"a hunter has patience. A hunter strategizes. A hunter knows where to go, what time of day, and what time of year would work best to get the bounty. A hunter works alone. I've been working on this farm for over four decades, and I got zero from your family. But a hunter knows that nothing comes easy...you have to work for what you want.

After your grandpa died and didn't leave me a stitch of land, I decided I would earn this farm. *My way.* I'd start with your dad. I planned for almost a year, knowing that fool would go out during hunting season by himself. He made it too easy. All I had to do was hide myself in the brush and shoot him. No one in town, not even the sheriff, suspected it was anything other than a freak accident. Case closed."

He paused for another moment and crossed his arms over his chest. Taking in another breath, he continued, "And then there were three. When it came to Alice, I knew she had cancer. Who knows how long she would have lived on if I hadn't intervened. I'm sure she'd probably be thanking me for taking that pain away. She didn't give me much fuss when I placed the pillow over her head in the middle of the night. No questions. Another case closed."

"Still, I didn't find the same satisfaction I feel when I snag a buck or a doe. You see, kid, a hunter *loves* the hunt. The thrill isn't the actual kill but the hunt itself and the anticipation of what is to come. That's when I decided to leave you alone for a while and watch you grow from a fawn to a buck. Only then would I get gratification watching you suffer. Then, and only then, would I get the exhilarating satisfaction I have been hoping for. While I waited for your mom to bleed out and die, I snuck in the house and left a note and that damn crucifix she was always so hell bent on wearing."

His mischievous smile grew as wide as a Cheshire cat's. He quickly walked out of the shed and around to the back. Brandon could hear his boots slosh in the mud with each step he took. The sound of his footsteps stopped briefly, and

174

then Brandon heard them start again, only this time they had slowed.

Brandon could feel his heart sinking to the pit of his stomach as the bile began to burn and rise up his esophagus like a volcano about to erupt. He started fussing with the rope that bound his wrists in hopes of somehow loosening it and setting himself free. It was useless.

A few seconds later, Evan appeared at the front door, pulling Maddie by the rope that was tied around her wrists. She wasn't moving. He climbed the single step into the shed and dropped Maddie next to Brandon's feet with a thud.

Brandon's eyes locked on her lifeless body, tears welling up in his eyes, as he silently begged for her to move or show signs she was breathing. She coughed as her body naturally moved from the side to her back on the floor, and blood sputtered out of her mouth and on to her face.

Brandon breathed a low sigh of relief, though he hated knowing the pain she was enduring. He quickly resumed fumbling with the ties behind his back while Evan lowered himself to his knees next to Maddie.

He stroked her blood-soaked hair out of her face to reveal the massive welt on her right eye. "Now there, little lady, it's time for your exit," he said, taking a hunting knife out of the back of his jeans. Her breath quickened at the sound of his voice, though her eyes remained closed.

Just then, Brandon felt something gently tug at the rope around his wrists. *A hand!* The touch of human fingers on his skin was unmistakable. He turned his head slowly, careful not to send Evan any alarms, but saw no one. The ropes abruptly loosened as if someone untied them.

His pulse quickened; he needed to act quickly. Brandon

contemplated his next move, careful to stay in the same position as if he were still bound, his eyes fixed now on Evan.

Evan took the knife in both hands and raised them above his head, looking straight down at Maddie's heart.

Brandon moved swiftly, dropping the ropes to the floor, grabbing the gun that Evan had left on the table next to him, and then swung around with his arm to deliver a blow to his head, knocking Evan off his knees and to the ground, the knife flying out of his hands and across the floor of the shed.

Brandon took two swift steps over to where Evan lay next to Maddie and without a word fired four shots into his body.

Brandon put the gun in his waistline and kneeled down beside Evan, placing his fingers on his neck for a pulse to make sure he was dead. Blood slowly began to pool from under Evan's body as he lay lifeless on the floor.

The monster was dead. The man that took Brandon's family from him was now gone forever.

Brandon quickly turned his attention back to Maddie. He pulled her away from Evan, who was only a few inches from her side.

"Maddie, please, don't leave me," he whispered to her, stroking her battered face gently with the back of his hand as she lay in his lap.

Maddie's eyes began to flutter open, the pain so over-whelming that it blurred her vision just a bit. "Brandon?" she called, her voice shaky.

"Yes! Maddie, it's okay! He's gone," he assured her, leaning down to place a kiss on her forehead. "The night-mare is over."

He breathed a sigh and looked ahead toward the floor where the rope had held him just minutes before.

"We're not alone, Maddie," he whispered, carefully moving her off his lap. He propped her up next to him with her back against the wall facing the chair and table.

Maddie turned to him and looked at him through her left eye, her right eye still swollen shut. Confused, she asked, "What do you mean?"

He glanced around the room, first looking at Evan's body just off to the side when something unexpectedly flashed just out of the corner of his eye, right behind the chair he had escaped just minutes before.

His mother's crucifix lay next to the rope that had bound him.

He nodded toward the gold necklace on the floor. "She's here with us."

Brandon stood up slowly and walked over to the necklace. He picked it up and gently put it back around his neck, running his fingers slowly down the sides of the chain before taking the cross in his hand and squeezing it with his right hand. He closed his eyes for a moment and sat in silence, knowing what he would find next. His eyes flittered open and, quietly working, he moved the chair and then the table. Maddie watched him, baffled by his sudden urge to move the furniture around in the shed instead of leaving. Once the furniture was situated in the corner, Brandon went to the edge of the area rug and pulled it back out of the way, careful not to disturb anything underneath.

And just like in his dream, he found the hidden door in the floorboards.

The door that had been built into the shed floor had a

small, rusted, gold pull ring. He gently slid his pointer finger into the ring and tugged slightly, pulling the door open to find her there. This perfect being, now a pile of bones lying in the cold, dark earth beneath them, lay peacefully, covered in a dirty tarp. Despite the mud and leaves that surrounded her, he could still envision her curly hair as black as a raven. As he reached down to touch her hands, which lay atop her chest, he imagined the once beautiful skin that enveloped her delicate bones. He could feel her smiling on him somehow.

"Be free now, Mom. Be free."

Chapter Thirty

The next morning, Brandon woke to the sun spilling in through the window. Maddie was asleep in the crook of his arm with her head resting on his chest. Her face was scraped and bruised but she still looked beautiful. He gently stroked her face, "You up? It's Thanksgiving." A sense of peace washed over him. The events over the last few days were finally in the rearview mirror and he could relax.

"Hey," she muttered with her eyes still closed. She stretched her arms over her head and winced, "ah!"

"You okay?"

"Yeah, just sore, but I have never felt better." Her eyes peered through her long lashes into his.

"Do you think you feel up to having Thanksgiving dinner today with Jimmy?"

She smiled at him. "Of course! We have so much to be thankful for. It's a must!"

Brandon kissed her on her forehead, careful not to put too much pressure on her fresh wounds. The paramedics were surprised at how lucky the two of them were. Despite the injuries to their heads and bodies, they walked away with a few bandages. No concussions. No broken bones. They walked away alive. It was a miracle, Brandon thought to himself. They were fortunate to be here. All of them.

The two of them took their time getting ready and had breakfast at the cabin before meandering over to the main house to see Jimmy around noon.

When Brandon walked in the door, Jimmy was already there waiting for them. He pulled Brandon in for a hug so tight, he thought his ribs may break.

"Easy Dad, I want to be able to enjoy my dinner," Brandon joked.

"Sorry, I'm just so damned happy to see you. You will never understand," he said. His eyes welled with tears as he flashed his warm smile. "And you! Maddie, come on over here."

She smiled back at him and walked over to join them in their hug. The three of them stood in the foyer embraced for a long minute before following Jimmy into the kitchen.

The house smelled of roasted turkey and stuffing. Jimmy had been prepping for hours. "Can we help you?" Brandon inquired as he poured them all glasses of wine.

"Nah, you two just go sit at the table and I'll bring this out. You need to rest those injuries," he replied.

Brandon and Maddie did not object. Their bodies were both still tired and would be sore for days to come. Jimmy joined them a few minutes later and took a seat at the head of the long dining table. The soft piano sounds of Phillip Glass filled the empty spaces in the room. Candlesticks were lit on the table and on the buffet behind them.

Jimmy lifted his glass for a toast. Brandon and Maddie joined him and lifted their glasses, too. "Today, we are thankful for each other, but especially thankful for Ella. If it weren't for her, we would not be sitting here today. Happy Thanksgiving to my one and only family. I love you both and I'm so grateful to be here with you."

"To Ella," they said in unison.

The three of them enjoyed their meal, never once mentioning the horror they had endured in the days before. Instead, they recounted old stories of their time on the farm when Brandon was a child. Jimmy shared his memories of Ella and Zach and how much love they had for each other and their excitement over being pregnant with Brandon. They ate and drank until they could feast no more. Savoring every morsel. Every word of conversation. Every second of their time together.

"Why don't we come back for Christmas?" Jimmy asked as he picked up the empty dishes from the table.

"Yeah, that sounds like a great idea, dad." He stood up and helped clear the table and get dessert. A thought stirred in the back of his mind while walked back to the kitchen. Evan was gone forever. There was nothing left for them to fear. But Brandon still had one last thing to do before heading back down to college. He needed to speak to the chief about Chad.

Brandon suspected he wasn't as innocent as everyone thought. His shed held contents that belonged to Ella and Brandon wanted them back. But not today. Tomorrow would be a new day and he could take care of it then.

Today, he would celebrate.

Chapter Thirty-One

A few weeks later, the three of them found themselves back at the farm. They sat in the living room, the fireplace roared with fresh flames. The room smelled of fresh pine from the Christmas tree. Outside, fresh snow had fallen the day before, leaving a blanket of white over every inch of the ground and trees.

With the last of the presents unwrapped and the paper strewn about, they sat and mindlessly watched the fire in the fireplace.

"So, have you made a decision about what you're going to do this semester?" Maddie asked, her head and hand resting on Brandon's chest.

Before Brandon could answer, a knock at the front door startled them. He jumped out of his seat and looked through the front window, his heart pounding.

It was a police car from town.

"It's okay, guys, let me get this," Jimmy said. He patted Brandon's shoulder has he passed by.

Brandon and Maddie quietly followed behind him.

Jimmy opened the door to see Chief Andrew standing there with held a box in his hand.

"Morning, Merry Christmas," Andrew followed and plastered a quick smile on his face.

Brandon let out a breath, realizing he had been holding it in the entire time. He couldn't handle any other dire news. Not for a while.

"Merry Christmas! All okay,?" Jimmy asked.

"Yeah, yeah, all is good. I wanted to bring this by to you." Chief Andrew handed Brandon a a small cardboard box, no larger than a shoebox, with his name plastered on the side in thick black marker.

Brandon gave him a baffled look. "What's this?"

"When you came to my office after we found your mother and told me about Chad, I looked into it." He looked at the box and then to Brandon. "You were right about him, son."

"Right about what?"

"He was stalking your mom. We found so much evidence in that shed. This box is just a few of the items that I can share with you right now. These are the unaltered pictures we found. I thought you might like to have them."

Brandon stared at the box. Maddie took a step toward him and placed her hand on his back.

"There is one more thing." Andrew hesitated for a moment. "I shouldn't be telling you this, but we did uncover other items that did not belong to your mother. He was actively stalking another woman in town. We arrested him yesterday evening and informed the woman. Because of you, she will be safe now. I don't know what he would have done, but I sure as hell was going to make the same mistake I did with your mom."

Maddie whispered, "You did it, Brandon." He turned to her and smiled before looking back to the chief.

"Thank you, Andrew." He rubbed his thumb over his name on the box. "Merry Christmas."

"Merry Christmas to all of you," the chief replied. He turned around and left. Jimmy closed the door behind him.

"You don't have to open that now, son, if you don't want to," Jimmy assured him.

"I do. It's okay." Brandon walked back into the living room and sat on the couch. Maddie sat next to him on one side and Jimmy sat on the other.

He opened the box to reveal the contents inside. The first picture he saw was of his mother, his dad, Jimmy, and Alice on the porch of the very house he sat in now. Their smiles forever memorialized.

Jimmy placed his hand on the corner of the picture to get a better look. "I remember this day, vividly. This was the day before your dad died. The last picture we ever took together. We had just finished bringing in the last of the tables for the party and were sitting on the porch drinking iced tea. We joked that it couldn't be a Long Island iced tea because your mom was pregnant."

"You know what this means, Brandon?" This means you are in this picture too!"

"You're right, I didn't even think of that!" Jimmy acknowledged.

"I can't think of a better gift to open today," Brandon said, tears welling up in his eyes.

Brandon took in a deep breath and relaxed farther into

the couch. Jimmy and Maddie did the same. The three of them spent time looking through pictures as Jimmy shared the stories he could remember of each one.

Minutes turned into hours and day into night, each of them sharing fond stories of their past as they ate and savored every second of the day.

Jimmy emerged from the kitchen at the end of the night and grabbed his jacket from the coat rack. "Do you guys need anything else before I head back over to the cabin for the night?" Jimmy asked as he walked toward the front door.

"No thanks, Dad," Brandon replied, getting up from the couch to join him in the foyer. "Are you sure you don't want to stay in this house with us? You don't have to stay in the cabin alone, you know?"

Jimmy smiled at him and pulled him in for a hug. "Nah. The cabin has a special place in my heart. I think I want to be there, if you don't mind."

"Sure thing, Dad," Brandon acknowledged and opened the door for him. He stepped out into the clear, cool winter night with Jimmy and stood on the porch as he watched Jimmy walk over to the cabin.

Once Jimmy got to the front porch, he turned and waved over to Brandon before entering the cabin for the evening. Brandon waved back and retreated into the warmth of his own house, turning off the lights inside, leaving only the twinkle of the Christmas lights on the tree and the glow from the fire to illuminate the room.

Maddie stood with Brandon next to the Christmas tree. "So, what do you think you'll do next?"

"I think I'm going to finish out the year at Penn." He took his hand and placed it under her chin, moving her face up to look at him. The bruises and cuts on her face were finally beginning to fade from deep purples to light yellow hues.

He couldn't believe that just over a month ago, they had faced death in the woods. The events of that day were still somewhat fresh on his mind, though he did his best to try and move past them. They had exhumed his mother's body and buried her at the family plot down the road. Brandon called in an excavator to come and bulldoze the shed down and remove every last bit of debris from the property.

He debated planting a garden where the shed once stood or just leave it be. One thing he knew for certain, it was time to move on. "I was thinking that once I graduate in the spring, I would pack up and move back up here," he said, his thumb caressing the side of her face. "I was hoping you would come and move in with me?"

She smiled and gently kissed his lips before relaxing her head back down on his chest. "I can't think of anywhere else I would rather be."

He sat back down on the couch, stretching his arm and legs out along its length. Maddie took his cue and lay down beside him, her body nestled into his open arm, her head resting back on his chest. They lay in silence in front of the fire, listening to the soothing sounds of its crackles and hisses, luring them into sleep.

Brandon found himself back in the middle of the field, just as he always had before the nightmare began. He caressed the tops of the wheat with his palms and noticed Maddie in the distance walking toward him. She was dressed in a white, flowing gown. When she arrived at his side, he pulled her in for a long hug, the gentle breeze blowing her hair off her shoulders. When he pulled away and looked back at the field, he noticed his mom and the end of a road that wasn't there before. She was waving at them to come to her.

They walked hand in hand to where his mother stood at the end of the road, opposite of where the shed used to be. She embraced them both as if saying *thank you*, a smile on her face, the cuts and dirt no longer on her body. She was beautiful. She stood back and motioned for them to keep going down the road. They continued walking, and when Brandon turned back, his mother was gone. The rays of the sun shone brightly on the spot where they had left her. This was it. Brandon somehow knew that he would never see her again.

He knew what he wanted to do. He looked to Maddie and knew this was the life he wanted. Her. This farm. And everything that came along with it.

For Brandon, the dream was just beginning.

A letter to my readers

Dearest Reader,

I hope you enjoyed reading this book as much as I enjoyed writing it. Please consider leaving a review. It's the greatest gift an author could ever hope for and it helps me grow as a writer.

Like many of you reading this, I am a mom with a full-time job who just wanted to pursue her passion. I wrote this book in the early hours of the morning and sometimes late hours of the evening after my kids went to bed. It took a few years, but was worth the effort and sleep deprivation.

A little insight into how this story came to be...

The setting in this story takes place in a town called Greenville, just outside of Port Jervis, New York. The Hudson Valley holds a special place in my heart and has been a staple in my life since birth. I have moved in and out of the area through the years and continue to be inspired by its beauty by day and haunted by its shadows at night.

This story began in my head as I rocked my youngest to sleep in his nursery. In the summertime, I would rock him with the window open and swear I could hear people screaming in the distance. (I later learned foxes make interesting noises in the middle of the night.) In the winter, I would rock him in that same chair and look at the creepy way the trees would move under the light of the moon. Funny things start to take shape in your mind when you are sleep deprived and staring out into the darkness. This story is a result of my wild imagination and lack of coffee. While the town itself is real, the characters and the places are a combination of many different made up ideas.

Thank you for taking the time to read my book! It means the world to me. Sweet dreams, readers.

Xoxo,

Mica

Acknowledgments

There are so many emotions I have and so much appreciation for those around me. I hope I can do them justice in this short space.

First, I would like to thank my husband, Dave. He has been my biggest cheerleader and is the best partner one could ever long for. I'm certain he would move the moon and stars for me if he knew it would make me happy. Babe, thank you for taking care of the boys when I needed to write, for encouraging me to keep going when I didn't want to, and for believing that I could do this. I love you and I hope I do for you all that you have done for me.

To my sons, Gabe and Cameron, I love you more than anything in the entire universe. You inspire me to be a better person and do great things in this life. Cameron, thank you for telling me I could do this and checking in mommy's book progress. And Gabe, thank you for answering all of my annoying texts about what font is best and how to navigate social media. You two are my reason.

Thank you to my parents, Shelagh and Pierre, who never stop pushing me to do what you knew I could do all along. You never gave up on me, even when I tried to give up on myself. I love you, Mom. I love you, Daddy. Thank you for always being there for me.

To my brother, JP, and his wife (and my bestie) Laura,

who I lovingly call Beanie. Thank you for supporting me and listening to me talk about this project for the last 4 years of my life. You're my support line and I love you both. Victory Lane! We got your book!

To all my beta readers who took the time to read my book and give me their honest feedback. I especially want to thank my Aunt Laura who was one of the first people I shared my first chapters with back in 2020. She gave me just the right amount of encouragement to keeping moving my story forward. And to my friend, Jenn Palenik, who not only read my book, but continued to nudge me to finish it through the last few years when I did not want to finish it at all. I'm lucky to have you in my life.

To my editor, Sara Kelly, who took a chance on a new writer and offered up her expert advice on how to take my story to the next level. You made the process so incredibly easy and I appreciate every minute that you spent providing feedback, copy edits and developmental edits. THANK YOU!

For all of my family and friends over the last few years who cheered me on and kept me going, thank you! I love you all from the bottom of my heart.

And most importantly thank you, Lord, for gracing me with this gift and for blessing my life with amazing people and incredible opportunities. Matthew 19:26

About the Author

Mica is a mom to two beautiful sons and wife to her best friend, Dave. This is her debut novella.

When she is not writing, she can be found cheering loudly at her youngest's soccer games, FaceTiming with her oldest when he's away at college, or sipping wine in the Gulf of Mexico with her sweetie.

Mica was born in New York and currently lives in Florida with her sons, husband, a black lab named Denver, and her grand fur-baby, a black cat named Oliver. She is lucky enough to escape the summer heat to return to the Hudson Valley each summer where she continues to find inspiration for her books.

facebook.com/micamerrillrice

instagram.com/micamriceauthor

Made in United States
Orlando, FL
15 November 2024

53933669R00125